Desperately Seeking Submissive

A 1Night Stand Collection

By
Landra Graf

Copyright © 2016 by Landra Graf
ISBN: 978-1-68361-020-5
Cover art by Tibbs Designs

Published by Decadent Publishing Company, LLC
Look for us online at:
www.decadentpublishing.com

What You Need

Dedication

To my besties, Lora, Monica and Lori, who read every draft, listened to every idea, and told me this was the one. To my husband, for always lifting me up. To three special ladies, who helped with the final steps and gave words of wisdom.

What You Need

A sexual submissive, Royce wants a woman who'll make his fantasies come true. The last thing he expects on his 1Night Stand is to be paired with Victoria, his ex-best friend. Haunted by their past, he refuses to deny his newfound attraction or his need for answers. This time, he doesn't plan to let her go.

Victoria has loved Royce forever, but the sting of his rejection is not so easily forgotten. No longer the naïve girl he knew, she's matured into a sexual dominant. This domme demands a chance to restart their relationship—on *her* terms. Knowing that one night will never be enough, she plans a seduction that will last forever.

Chapter One

A simple knock would grant him entrance to a suite in one of the most expensive hotels in the tri-county area. Royce clutched his canvas bag and stared at the room number plate. According to Madame Eve, a beautiful woman stood behind the barrier, one who could make all his fantasies come true. He had plenty of ideas rattling around in his head, and being with a gorgeous woman who accepted his desires would make the night perfect. He rocked on the balls of his feet, checked the time on his phone again, then put it on silent mode before another e-mail could chime through. Seven o'clock, time to...*shit*. He didn't sleep with random women. Not now, not ever. But dominant women weren't popping up around the corner and he'd paid for this.

Fuck it.

He rapped his knuckles on the heavy wood. Three solid taps. The door swung open slowly, revealing too much beauty to absorb at once, and his mouth dried. Red stilettos with tiny spikes all over them, legs that went on and on to lush curves, a short and sexy red dress, and gorgeous black hair. The dimmed hallway lights and non-existent ones in the room obscured her face, but that didn't stop the jolt of pure lust, not helped by two years of celibacy, that speared straight to his cock. Without a word, she grabbed his tie, its black a stark contrast to her porcelain white, elegant fingers, and pulled him into the room. The latch clicked into place behind him and his bag fell to the floor when she shoved him against the cold, firm surface. Goose bumps rose on his skin along with the hairs on the back of his neck.

"Hi." About the only word he managed before a pair of luscious, plump red lips descended on his. One sharp heel spike scratched the skin above his ankle. His trousers were tight and rough on his thighs, igniting a pleasurable pain in his pulsing erection. She molded her body to his, and her nibbling bites on his mouth sent his brain reeling. The press of her weight sparked his nerves. Lord, he hadn't experienced anything like that.

Skin hot and flushed, he moved to embrace her and deepen the kiss. Instead, she grabbed his wrists and anchored them above his head; a simple gesture of dominance and one he'd never thought of as arousing until then. Her ministrations slowed to a crawl, as she opted for tracing the seams of his lips. He thrust his own eager tongue forward, desperate for another taste of spice and something familiar...a flavor of summer and sweet lemonade.

She pressed harder, her breasts crushed to his chest, his wrists still restrained, her nails biting into the flesh. Royce's desire ratcheted up further. As he thought he might succumb to the most embarrassing release ever, she pulled away.

Panting, he tugged at his shirt collar. His date faced the window, out of the fan of illumination from low-lit lamps within the room. Curvy with toned arms and legs, her bare back on display, she stood straight and confident, her profile nothing less than stunning.

He took a deep breath and exhaled hard. *What a way to start the night.* Chemistry wouldn't be an issue. But he also wanted a little conversation.

"That's some way to say hello." Chuckling, he grabbed his discarded bag and moved farther into the room.

"Yes, it is. But I've wanted to do that for a long time." Her voice sounded sultry and all-too-familiar.

Holy fuck.

"Tori?"

"It's Victoria nowadays." She turned away from the window. "How's life, Royce?" Her dark brown eyes appeared black and the desire in them reminded him of the erection from hell he still sported. She looked nothing like he remembered. Her long hair was gone, replaced with a bob, and no longer a radical shade of pink or blue. Baggy clothes to cover her figure were obviously a thing of the past.

"How?" He'd just had an extremely arousing moment stuck between a solid surface and his ex-best friend. *Stop thinking about sex.* Tally that under the unexpected column. He ran his fingers through his hair. "Where the fuck have you been?"

Tori, or Victoria—whatever she called herself—bit her lip, a nervous habit she'd always had to avoid a topic or feared how her next words would be received, although right then it made him remember the things she'd done with her teeth to him a minute before. "I've been around."

"That's all I get after eight years of the silent treatment? We were best friends, prom dates, peaches and cream. You give me nothing and then kiss me like—" He cut off, not wanting to let his arousal become a verbal statement.

"Like what?" She sounded intrigued and playful. It pissed him off, like she didn't care about his feelings.

Brutal truth, meet open air.

"Like you want to fuck me until I can't think straight."

Tori's mouth spread into a wicked grin. "Really? So, no more thinking I'm only friend material then? No running away now that you know it's me?"

"I'm not like you. I can handle a bit of an embarrassment and stick around."

"Oh, you call our first kiss a little embarrassment." She stepped toward him, tucking a chunk of her short, dark brown hair behind her ear. "I'd say baring my soul and confessing my love to the person I was closest to and then being told no, in so many words anyway, was more than little humiliating. I think I deserve some retribution, and your pitching a tent seems small in comparison. I also wouldn't be so quick to call that kiss just now embarrassing. Judging by your pants, you agree."

Damn. Clenching his fists, he willed himself to calm the fuck down. "I'd like to think you know me better than that. You'd been drinking that night. I don't get involved with someone under the influence. You threw me off guard."

Not to mention he'd been unable to admit his submissive nature to her back then, but he didn't want to go back down the sex road. Not yet, anyway.

"If I remember correctly, you weren't one for one-night stands either. I can see that's changed."

"Not entirely. I don't expect...a quick screw, but some conversation. Something beyond physical stimulation." He waved a hand toward the door, wanting to change the subject to something a little safer. Like why she never bothered to talk to him since that night. "Tori, did you think I wasn't going to apologize the next day? Hell, I did. In a text. In a voice mail."

"I never got the messages. I changed my number first thing in the morning."

The words tore at the wound of their split, cracking it wide open again.

"Why in the hell would you do that?" His voice rose in anger. "Where the fuck did you get off?"

Her eyes flashed, and in two quick strides she stood before him, resting a gentle palm on his cheek, the other cupping his erection. "Don't ever raise your voice at me again or I'll make sure you're hurting and not in the good way. Also, my name is Victoria," she whispered.

"I'm sorry. It's—"

"I'm sorry, too." She stroked his straining cock. "I'm going to make it up to you. We can save the questions for later. That is, if the rest of you is up to it?"

His Tori would never have acted like that. The woman before him appeared more confident and assertive in her sensuality. The sole similarity between the two lay in the mischievous look her eyes held, and the fact he wouldn't fight her. The one time he'd refused something she'd asked of him, she'd disappeared from his life.

"How do you plan to make it up to me?" In a hotel room with a hot, dominant woman...he couldn't summon the words to tell her to stop. Not that he wanted to.

Leaning in, she placed a sweet kiss on him, then pulled back an inch. "You'll see."She went to work loosening his tie and removing it from his neck. His mind raced with possibilities.

"What are we go—"

"Shhh. Half the fun of an experience is the mystery and wonder of what will happen. Trust me." She slipped the loop of the tie around one wrist and moved behind him, securing his arms behind his back. *Holy hell.* She planned to tie him up; something he never would have expected from his childhood playmate.

"I'd be fine with a simple conversation."

"But I owe you so much more than that." She wrapped her arms around his chest. The spike heels made her tall enough to rest her head on his shoulder. Seconds of anticipation passed, then a hot breath, coupled with a swipe of liquid heat on his ear lobe. Victoria unbuckled his belt. He shuddered.

"See, Royce, you need some assistance." At the mercy of her *assistance*, he hoped it ended with release. "Now, I'm going to do a few things. I want you to feel them."

Dipping beneath the band of his boxer briefs, she gripped his cock and drew him free. The rush of semi-cold air in the room and the heat of her palm had him jerking in response. "Vic—"

"Hush now. Don't talk. Just feel. And if you come before I tell you to, this will be the first and last thing we do together this evening. I'll kick you out before you even get your dick back in your pants. Nod if you understand."

Royce obeyed and she stroked gently, then firmly. When he shivered, she fondled his balls, keeping him on edge, her efforts both heavenly and maddening. Bound the way she desired, he didn't dare speak, fearing she'd stop her ministrations.

He bit the inside of his cheek to stifle his groans, but when she cupped his balls and tightened her grip around his shaft, a moan tore loose. Victoria circled and dropped to her knees in front of him. Snaking her tongue out, she traced up and down both sides of his cock. As she laved at the pre-cum from the tip, he rose on the balls of his feet toward her hot breath.

She glanced up, light catching the deep golden flecks in her eyes, her expression beautiful and determined. She flicked the tip of his cock with one finger, the pain a sharp contrast to the earlier pleasure of her tongue. A perfect balance. "I think for all the trouble you've put me through, you deserve to be cold-cocked."

Standing, she dragged his pants partially up with her and backed him into one of the four bedposts. "Hold onto that. You'll need the support."

Royce wrapped his hands around the post as best he could. The cool wood felt good against his heated skin. Victoria had him more aroused then he'd ever been.

She shifted from the table next to the TV, and slipped something between her lips. Sinking to the carpet in front of him, she grabbed his cock and inserted him into her warmth. Extreme cold and heat surrounded his cock in heaven and agony. *Ice.* His climax neared and he gripped the post for dear life. The pressure built as the ice melted and she sucked. He needed release: soon.

Leaning back, she began to piston her hand around his cock. "Come. Now."

The words were the final push he needed, and his balls clenched. He watched, mesmerized by the sight of his cum jetting into her mouth, and shuddered through the final release. His vision blurred.

She swallowed and licked her lips. "You can let go of the post now."

He collapsed.

"Oh, hell. Royce? Are you okay?" Victoria went to her knees. His pulse ran a little fast. She ruffled his hair, hoping to see a change in his closed eyes, praying she didn't hurt him or make an error.

Then reaching behind him, she removed the tie around his arms. "Get up."

With her tender touch on the side of his cheek, he started to move, his skin damp and cold compared to hers.

"Tori...." Royce attempted to sit up on his elbows then fell back again. "Crap. Sorry about that."

"Can you stand?" Standing, she leaned over to help him up." Actually, give me a minute. I just need a drink." He squinted and beads of sweat formed on his brow, his skin unnaturally pasty.

"Hold on." She'd forgotten about Royce's hypoglycemia. He'd

been that way since they were kids, always needing at least a snack every couple of hours. "When's the last time you ate?"

He blinked several times. "Around lunchtime.

"Have anything in that duffle of yours?"

"A protein bar in the left pocket."

"Stay still." Victoria shot to his bag and dug in the side pocket, found the snack, and helped him peel back the wrapper. "And here I thought all this fainting stuff was because I blew your mind."

"Still good at the bad jokes, I see." He nibbled.

"Yes, always good at bad jokes. Now, how about I order us some real food?"

While chewing, he tucked his cock back in his pants with his free hand. His actions were slow and controlled, hands steady due to the carbs, normal color back in his cheeks. "Don't think you can continue to postpone our detailed conversation with food. I can't be bribed."

Victoria grinned at how delicious he appeared: his brown hair in disarray, pants loose and unbuttoned, food muffling the words. He seemed younger in the candlelight, a near, spitting image of the teenage boy she'd embraced in a beat-up Honda CRX. "I think I remember you could be bribed easily if it involved Philly cheesesteak and peach cobbler." She walked to the cabinet and poured him a glass of water.

"Fine, I'll agree to the food, but I want to discuss the last eight years over dinner." He straightened his shirt the best he could, the fabric nearly see-through with sweat. He wouldn't relent. The lone dominant part of Royce had always been his stubbornness when resolving arguments or during tough conversations. If she truly didn't want to talk about it, she could make him quit asking, but it wouldn't be fair. No doubt he'd weasel his way into discussing their past one way or another.

She extended the glass to him, the touch of his skin clammy like his cheek had been.

"Okay. I'll order and we can talk."

"Sounds great." He took a drink, passed back the glass, and stood to button his pants. "I never knew you were into D/s."

"I never knew you were into it either, but I'm fairly new to the scene."

"The profile I got from Madame Eve said as much. What got you started?" He took a couple of small steps away from the bed, appearing steady on his feet.

"Things...." she hedged, setting his water on a cabinet, then gestured toward the bathroom. "How about a shower while we wait for dinner?"

"You don't have to be afraid to tell me things. We used to tell each other everything."

"I know. I need a little bit longer to get comfortable with discussing the past with you. It's been a long time since one of our heart-to-hearts." She sat on the bed. "I'm afraid you won't look at me the same." She didn't do deep conversation with anyone except her therapist. With friends and family, she kept her conversations playful and away from the topic of her personal life and feelings. "I also don't do pity parties."

Royce shifted in close and took her right hand in his. "It's not a pity party. It's a conversation. Big difference. You don't need my sympathy or compassion. I want to know where you went and what you've been up to. I think I deserve that much."

"Yes, you do. And more." She sighed and laced her fingers with his.

He pressed a gentle kiss to them then let go, heading to the bathroom. "How about you ask me questions? I'm not an interrogator, and I'm sure you want to know what I've been up to."

There he went again, always wanting to make her comfortable with every situation. "Do you always have to try to make me feel better? Feel safe?" She trailed him to the bathroom, pausing outside the door.

"That's what friends do and I never stopped thinking of you as one. So, I'm going to shower and you can stand right here and ask me questions." He smiled then closed the door partially. Victoria, like a voyeur, longed to peek around the edge of the obstruction. In their current circumstance, did etiquette demand she give him privacy?

"Oh, shit."

"What?" Victoria inched closer, ready to enter the room when the door opened. Her gaze connected with a gorgeous, muscled chest, smattered with brown hair. Perfect.

"I forgot my bag."

A bag? She struggled to focus on his words. She still possessed all the arousal from their earlier escapade, and his naked, toned torso with its perfect pecs didn't help. "No problem. I'll get it."

Heading for the duffle, she searched for anything to get her focus off her horny-as-hell body. Question time. "So what have you been up to since college, Royce?"

"I graduated, received the Bachelor's in Marketing I wanted. I got a job with a good company in the area and I'm a manager now."

Holding the bag, she wheeled around and caught Royce's vacant expression. Something about his response rang false. "Tell the truth. This is me you're talking to."

He laughed. "I hate it. The job. Playing babysitter to a bunch of people. I mean, not all the employees are bad. It's the fact I'm not the hard-ass meant for the role. Upper management likes to think I am, but I don't think my employees are fooled."

"Why don't you quit?" She extended the duffle toward him.

"It's not that easy. The job pays the bills and I'm responsible for more than just me."

Her stomach tightened. She'd specifically requested someone with no attachments. "A kid?"

"No. Aunt Maude."

"You mean you're still at home?" The thought terrified her. Victoria wouldn't be caught occupying the same space as her own family for more than thirty minutes. The tightness disappeared, and she gave a silent thanks. If there'd been a woman or child waiting for him, she would've been...devastated? The thought sent nervousness creeping back into her gut.

"Are you going to be like everyone else?" Royce looked her over, eyebrow raised. She'd obviously hit a nerve.

"Like how?"

"Judging me for living at home? I get grief from a few co-workers, some of the neighbors. People think I can't make it on my own, in my own place."

She shrugged. "They're assholes." But she wanted to know the reason. Though she'd been surprised to hear he still lived at home, he must have one.

"Maude had a stroke about a year ago. I moved in to be there for her. Especially after Grandma—"

"Grandma?" Victoria's shoulders slumped. Royce's grandmother had acted as her second mom—a supportive mom. Her decisions to cut those close to her out of her life had come with too many painful costs.

"She had a heart attack. Maude was outside and I didn't make it in time. Bottom line: after the stroke, I needed to be there as much as I could be. I don't want to risk not having a chance to say good-bye."

She brushed his cheek. "I understand." Then she leaned in and kissed him. The duffle between them made things awkward, but she wanted to convey her apologies. He'd never been given a chance to say good-bye to her, either, and any guilt she held could be laid at her feet along with her misguided justifications about keeping her friend in the dark about her life.

He pulled back and gave a small grin, part innocence and part pure delight: a magical picture. God, she wished she could bottle those smiles.

"I'm going get that shower now." He shut the door, his need for privacy obvious. The night wouldn't be simple. At all.

She plopped onto the bed with a sigh. The soft mattress and satin sheets were cool next to her bare back, a balm to soothe the internal freak-out. She was in deep. If the pre-shower blow job and conversation gave any indication of how the night would go, mindless sex would be placed at the bottom of the list. Every moment she spent with Royce gave him another chance to make her stern resolve never to cry again over the past crumble. She eased her feet out of the high heels.

One night. She needed to remember that. Nothing more than a chance to act out the fantasy she'd always held close to her heart. But the surprise of a lifetime; Royce wanted her, sexually. Back in college, the fantasy involved a sweet night under the stars with a bit of wild picnic fun. Not the pure erotic pleasure she got from restraining him and watching the look of desire glaze over his eyes, with his cock at her mercy, while he gripped the bedpost. *Damn.*

The memory of her last stay came unbidden. Victoria jumped from the bed as the shower came on and grabbed the room service book on the desk. Being alone with her thoughts let the memories of the forced intercourse, bruises and marks along her body, and the fake apologies the asshole had given about having too much to drink surface. She flipped through the menu pages, forcing the awful recollection away. Stuck between anxiousness, the butterflies in her stomach, and arousal that wouldn't subside, she needed release. The best solution: get some relief before answering Royce's questions.

Chapter Two

"**H**ey Vic—" Royce caught sight of Victoria on the bed— her head thrown back, dress hiked, legs spread, and a pair of fingers rubbing her clit—and he forgot what he'd started to say. His cock rose to immediate attention behind his silk lounge pants. Somehow, seeing her completely uninhibited by his presence aroused him as much as her restraining him had.

"Come here." Her voice, low and husky, filled him with a need to please her. To bring her to the same satisfaction she'd brought to him. Yet, their plans were changing again.

Moving forward, he sat next to her, sliding his thumb to mingle with her moist heat, her juices coating it. "I thought we were going to talk."

"Oh." She moaned and pushed her hips forward. "Yes, talking is in the plan, but right now, Royce, I need your mouth on my pussy. No argument. You want to know about anything prior to tonight, you're going to have lick me."

Goose flesh broke out on his arms. The tantalizing scent of her arousal hung in the air between them, a summer breeze mixed with spice. "I'd be honored."

He'd experienced his most comfortable sexual moments since entering the room. There lay a chance to reward her for them and create more. He spread her legs further.

"Stop," Victoria said, her arm a sudden barrier between his face and her clit.

He halted. *What the hell?*

"Lie down first." A smile played over her lips. She planned something devious. Something involving two pieces of silk fabric half the length of him dangling from her grip.

"All right." He fell back.

"Is this what you meant by ordering room service?" Royce asked with a grin.

She laughed, tying his first wrist to the headboard behind him. "Consider this an appetizer."

"I never thought it would be like this with you."

"What do you mean?" She secured the second fabric strip until both hands were firmly tied to the headboard.

"Every minute is more exciting and surprising then the last. You're not afraid of taking action, and I feel comfortable, not awkward."

She beamed. "I'm glad you like everything so far. But you've had some experience before, right?"

Normally he would've avoided bringing up his failed BDSM situations, but he wanted her to know everything. Hiding things wouldn't make conversation between them any easier and she needed to know he wouldn't be afraid of words, of confessions.

"My last experience ended with the woman running from my house, calling me a pervert, and leaving me handcuffed to my bed without the key."

"That's horrible." She caressed his cheek and swung one leg over his chest. "Seems you've had a run of bad luck. I can't say I've been any luckier in the scene. I think things are looking up tonight though. You need to pick a safeword."

Safeword. He'd chosen one long ago, but had never needed to use it. It wouldn't work in their situation anyway. "My safeword is Tori."

"What?" Her process of straddling his body halted. "My nickname is your safeword?"

Did his confession offend her? Regardless, he wouldn't apologize for his feelings or the truth. "Yes, it is. Back when I'd first decided to learn more about me and the whole D/s scene, I was instructed to pick a word I associated with feeling safe. One that wouldn't be confusing to others. I'd always felt safe with you."

She pulled away and sat beside him.

Unloading everything on her when she'd been seeking release could be viewed as an asshole move. Yet, eight years had provided plenty of perspective to think about Victoria and what she'd meant to him. Losing her, letting her cut off their friendship, had eaten a hole in his heart. The hole seemed to be healing with each passing minute and every word shared, but he'd need more than a blow job and halfhearted conversation to seal the deal. The guys would call him a bitch for being so in tune with his feelings. *Fuck it.* He didn't care. She needed to know the importance of their friendship, to know what she meant to him.

"I won't apologize for telling you how I feel, but it's true. You saved me from the awkwardness of school dances, mentored my first date, and made me feel like I was normal when I didn't have a father around to guide me through manly pursuits. Hell, Victoria, you taught me how to shave."

She put her back to him. Head shaking, she exhaled, whether in disbelief or anger, he couldn't tell.

He tugged at the restraints, but his arms didn't budge. Damn, he needed her to look at him. "Please say something. I'm not trying to make this evening uncomfortable, but I can't lie to you. I've never been able to."

"When I'm trying to keep this night tear-free...." She regarded him with wet tracks on her cheeks. "When I think I've got you figured out, you blow a hole in my understanding of us. This whole evening, you've been doing that. Tonight is about enjoying the possibilities of intimacy...sex, between us. Hell, I can't believe you stayed, and I don't want to waste the opportunity." Her next words were barely above a whisper. "I told you I wouldn't avoid this conversation, but right now?"

When she faced him once more, fear had entered her eyes. He didn't know where it came from, but he wanted to get rid of it. He also hoped he wasn't responsible for her fear. His gut clenched at the possibility. Prodding her for a reaction wouldn't work. He kept insisting on explanations and words to assuage his emotions of being away from her so long. "I'm sorry. What can I do to make it up to you?"

She wiped the moisture from her cheeks. "Be patient. Let me get us back on track and plan on never having to use that safeword." Determination and authority laced the reply, her words a decree, not a suggestion.

Victoria took a deep breath. Torn between arousal and a rising fear of what Royce would think about her confessions and her decisions following his rejection, she wanted to use the release to forget. Every moment spent in his company proved her heart wouldn't pass the night unscathed. He didn't seem to get it, didn't seem to understand he'd been her world, her lodestone up until the rejection. "Close your eyes."

Royce followed her directions, lowered his lids and wet his lips. A fresh rush of liquid moistened her clit. Reaching release would be her reward, and she'd be damned before his feelings would wound her or keep her away from completion. She refused to let pain over her past decisions interfere with the moment either. He needed to pay her back for dragging up orgasm-reducing memories.

"Consider this the expense for your confession and taste." She straddled his head, lining her pussy with his mouth to receive his services. The first lap of his tongue sent a shudder up her spine. She stopped short of vocalizing how good it felt, but that didn't stop Royce. His low groan of pleasure echoed through her body and he twisted his head, nipping at the inside of her thigh.

She laced her fingers with his and ground her pussy against his mouth. He began a fast, in-and-out motion with his tongue. With every lift of her hips, he flicked her clit. If he kept going, it would be over in minutes. Lifting away from his face, she watched him move his head, stretching his neck in a desperate attempt to connect with her center again.

"Should I allow you the pleasure of my orgasm?"

"Please," Royce begged. "I need it."

Victoria chuckled. "*You* need it?"

"Yes. I would kill to taste you again. Delicious."

The words were exactly what she needed to hear, the strain in his voice making her want to draw out the torture a little longer. He still kept his eyes closed, and a pout formed on his lips. To drive that look, the craving he had for her release, ignited frenzy in her blood. He amazed her, wanting her in any way she deigned to give. She sat on his face again, and he returned to licking, nibbling, and worshipping her pussy until she arched her back. Her mind blanked with the force of her release. Legs locked and numb, she tried to sustain the feeling of sensual abandon. She growled as he made another assault on her sensitized flesh and a jolt of pure bliss raced through her. *This is divine.*

She barely possessed enough strength to untie Royce's bonds before sinking onto the bed beside him. Sated and still in the afterglow, she stretched out on the satin sheets. She wanted the rest of the night to feel that way; no deep emotion, just the pure wonder of release, and the endorphins that came with it. So why did she feel a sudden tug of hurt when he rose from the bed without looking at her? Refusing to give into an evaluation of the feelings, she turned to her side, ready to issue another command to her one-night submissive.

"Roy—" A knock at the door cut her off.

***

Royce mumbled a thank-you to the hotel employee and shut the door fast. He eyed the trays that lined the serving cart along with a pitcher of water and a couple of Bud Lights. "What did you order?"

"Our favorites." Victoria's melodic voice floated through the bathroom door, a definite ego boost for his oral skills. "Fried pickles. Caesar salad. Prime rib with loaded baked potatoes."

His stomach rumbled. They were their favorites all right. Another thing that made them a perfect fit: similar food tastes.

Perfect fit? He pushed the thought aside. Perfect friends maybe, but forgiving the last eight years would take more than oral sex and delicious food.

He lifted the dome off a serving platter, revealing an abundance of fried dill slices and a bowl of ranch dressing in the center. "Damn, they smell delicious. Vic, you have to try one."

He dipped one in the dressing then touched the battered goodness with his tongue to ensure they weren't too hot. A crunch of seasoned breading and thin-sliced pickle greeted his taste buds, as much of an aphrodisiac as Victoria's arms rubbing his shoulders when she stepped beside him. Dunking another pickle, he brought it to her mouth. A quick nip with her teeth and the treat disappeared, but not before a dribble of ranch fell between her breasts. His cock began to stir as she gently sucked his fingers. Answering her challenge, he leaned down to lick and taste the spot where the sauce had landed.

"I'm ready for something sweet." She moaned. "Luckily, I'm dessert."

"At the rate this is going, we'd better slow down." Royce smiled at the light blush on her skin. "I'd hate for the food to go cold."

"Always thinking with your stomach."

"Not this time." Sliding his arms around her waist, he pulled her close, loving how her body molded to his.

But half the night had passed and they'd only skimmed the surface of his fantasies. Anger over the past or not, he wanted to see the date through to the end. Wanted to explore the lengths of the desire he couldn't deny. "I think we need to replenish our energy, and you're going to need plenty if you're my dessert."

Chapter Three

Stuffed. The only word to describe her belly. Every morsel Royce fed her tasted delicious, and unless he gave her a bite first he didn't get one: a wonderful game. Victoria had taken advantage of flicking his chest with her mini flogger across the little dining table every time he licked his fingers or presented a bite of something she didn't want. But anger never entered his eyes, just pure lust, desire, and something else she didn't want to identify. He seemed more keyed up as the meal went on, until she became too full to continue.

He ate freely, savoring each bite, and she wished for a larger stomach. A ton of food still remained.

She crossed her legs, allowing her robe to droop open and show her nude body underneath. "Have you always known?"

"My submissive preferences?"

"Yes."

"I don't think I thought of them in the sexual realm, but I wasn't like other guys. I didn't want to fight like little boys do. I was more concerned with getting along with others and having friends. Why?"

Victoria laughed. "I remember you always wanted to play cops and robbers, except I had to play the robber because you wanted to be the bank manager getting tied up."

"I enjoyed every situation where you took control. I was more than happy to follow along." He stuffed a bite of baked potato into his mouth.

Yes, happy to follow along until she'd tried to kiss him at the college party. He'd driven her home out of friendly duty and then she took things to a level he couldn't commit to.

"So, your proclivities were why you pushed me away?"

"Yes, partially," he whispered. A swig of beer, another forkful of food, and she waited for his response, though she wanted to demand it. "I said some horrible things I wish I hadn't, but you were more experienced then I was in the sexual game. Sure, I knew the basic mechanics, but I couldn't sustain arousal with simple foreplay and an insertion routine. To admit those things to you would've been beyond embarrassment, or make you think I was some disgusting pervert."

She snorted. "Really? Maybe you don't realize what you were to me."

But looking back, she understood the reason for his rejection. Admitting his true persuasion would've been difficult. Hell, he'd probably refused to embrace it any further at that point.

"What do you mean?" He set the utensils down and twisted toward her. She had his *full* attention now.

"Senior year, you were my prom date, and as soon as Betsy Crain appeared, you abandoned me. I let my cherry get popped that night by Scott the Jock. That summer, when you blew me off for the movies with another chick, I spent time with some random dude I met at the drive-in. Every encounter. Every night in another guy's arms happened after you deserted me for someone else." She paused and took a deep drink of liquid courage. Setting the bottle on the table, she summoned the strength as the dominant to meet his eyes. "The worst part is that every moment, kiss, touch, and screw, I couldn't get through unless I thought it was you."

"Damn." He pushed his chair back, looking anywhere, everywhere, but at her.

"Don't you back away from me again."

His back snapped straight. "I'm sorry."

"For what?"

"For telling you I didn't want to be another fuck." He rose from his chair and kneeled before her. "For never realizing your true feelings or bothering to trust you enough to know all my dirty secrets. Pushing you away and telling you I didn't need a drunken girl throwing herself at me for the fun of it seems like the rudest fucking thing I could've said. I'll take any punishment."

Victoria stroked the feathers under his chin. "Your apology is enough. You can get up now."

She breathed easy as he positioned himself back in his chair and returned to the meal. Her longest held secret had been confessed. Talking about the other unsaid parts of their time apart shouldn't have been so hard. His sincerity and pained gaze, paired with the apology, awakened hope for something beyond that night. *You're keeping things simple remember? Focus on lighter conversation and the present.*

"I kicked the crap out of Betsy when she tried to tell me you sucked in bed."

Royce looked up from his plate. "What? When?"

"After you ditched your virginity to her during senior year."

"Shit, that's funny. She gave me a second chance when I took her to my office Christmas party two years ago, which followed with the unfortunate handcuff incident."

"You didn't." She giggled. "Who found you?"

He winced. "Grandma and Aunt Maude. Not my finest moment."

"I'd say not. Give me a bit of dessert, please." She closed her eyes and waited to receive the treat, marveling at how easy and comfortable they were together even after the years apart. To be able to share anything, any thought, without judgment. Instead of a sweet, he gave her a chaste kiss and pulled back before she could initiate a more thorough connection.

"So, eight years to account for. What have you been up to?" he asked, cutting another piece of beef for himself. He seemed more focused on his plate than her. No doubt to stay on topic.

"Working mostly. Got my degree, a liberal arts deal. I didn't have my mind set back then and it definitely bit me in the ass." She paused to gauge his response, hoping he caught the double entendre. He stopped eating. Teasing her way through the conversation would make the talking easier. "I've got a good job, too. I'm an office manager for a local business. Nothing spectacular, but I'm appreciated and I like my bosses."

"What about living arrangements? House? Apartment?" he asked.

"Apartment, out west of Bentonville. Keeps me within a decent driving distance to work. No pets. No time for them."

Royce lifted one eyebrow. "And that's it?"

"I lead a pretty boring life. What were you expecting, some secret dominatrix career or something?" Victoria sat up and slapped her flogger on the table.

"No need to get upset, but I don't buy it. You say that's it, but what about Motorcycle Hot Rod Guy?" Royce had always been blunt, especially with family and friends. That trait hadn't changed with time.

"He was gone pretty quick. A dime a dozen." She propped her arms up and stared out the window at the twinkling lights. *Please let it go.*

"Your mom said you'd married him." Royce's voice held a note of pain.

God. He knows I'm lying. Stomach in knots, she closed her eyes for a moment.

"She told Aunt Maude, who of course asked me why I hadn't received an invite to the wedding. It's pretty sad when you have to tell your family your best friend wants nothing to do with you. I also know you divorced four years ago." His words were laced with pain and she didn't know how to respond.

"Oh, Royce." She opened her eyes again and put her hand on his. He jerked away and the loss of connection hurt. Her throat tightened.

"No. I'm not going to sit here and get shut out again. I won't be lied to for the sake of embarrassment or fear. Remember I already did that stupid shit and it didn't get us anywhere." He stood and began to pace. "Or is it that I'm not worth your confidence? Not worth sharing secrets with anymore? I've given you what you wanted. Proved that I see you as a woman and I would gladly let you fuck me until I die of a heart attack or lose all feeling in my legs. I want you."

He paused, yanking at his brown hair, his skin flushed red. She'd fucked up. Even after her myriad of bad choices, she'd loved him and longed to be with him. Imagined him when she touched her pussy in the early morning hours when she couldn't sleep. Treating him like another submissive looking to get laid for mutual pleasure had been a big mistake.

Royce stared at her with tears on his face. "I don't know what you want from me, Victoria."

She jumped out of her seat and went to him. His beautiful face blurred as her eyes welled up. "I'm sorry. So damn sorry. I...yes, I was married. Yes, it was Motorcycle Man. And he beat me." Her shoulders shook, and she dropped her head, not wanting to see his face or answer more questions. Finally, she said, "I got pregnant, exactly one week after you rejected me. I hid it...for a month." Sobs came, unbidden.

"Vic—"

"No! I'm not finished. Let me get this out." She sniffled and swallowed to get rid of the lump lodged in her throat. "We did the shotgun Arkansas wedding bit. Everything was okay. He drank a bunch. I didn't. He'd leave for a few weeks and then come back. I thought it would get better once the baby came. I dropped out of college, didn't want you or anyone else to know. And then...."

She couldn't help it; the tears ran in earnest.

"What happened?" Royce wrapped his arms around her shoulders. The movement arrested the sudden urge to collapse on the floor.

She wiped her cheeks. "About six months into the pregnancy, he brought home another woman. We fought and he pushed me down the stairs. And that was the end of my daughter."

"Oh, sweetie." Royce dragged her into a hug. Her tears and anguish came out as a loud, sobbing mess as she rested her head on his bare chest.

Minutes passed and he stroked her hair until she stilled.

"You left him, I take it?" he asked, keeping his voice calm and soft.

"No. I stayed like an idiot, addicted to pain pills, too depressed to fight. He would bring in his friends for parties, and I would—"

"Shh, you don't have to say anymore." Hell, he didn't want to hear any more. The whole situation broke his heart and he felt horrible for being too damn selfish and oblivious so long ago. Things would have been different. Maybe. Maybe not. He wanted to find the piece-of-shit ex who'd used her like baggage and string him up in a dark dungeon where Royce could beat him until the man didn't know his own name. Excessive yes, but avenging the woman he loved would be worth it. She was one of the most important people in his life. Of course he loved her. Love between friends. And nothing more, right?

Victoria leaned back. "I've made a real mess of things, haven't I?"

"I think we both have."

"So much for a sexy dinner. Sorry for letting a waterfall loose on your chest."

He grinned. "It's fine. I think I contributed some of it. Besides, I'm good for it—listening, comforting, the whole thing. I can be what you need me to be."

He damn well meant it, too. The *love* word popped in his head again. Yes, he loved her. He'd always loved her, but until that night, the emotion stayed tied to friendship, not sex and intimacy. But desire beat strongly within him and he longed to explore all the possibilities their night presented.

"Here, let me get you cleaned up." She grabbed a napkin from the table, but her attempt to evade the subject wouldn't work.

He flung his arm to intercept her, but she moved it out of the way and pinned it behind his back with one hand then gently wiped away the moisture on his chest with the other. A rush of renewed arousal coursed through him.

She sighed. "I love your body. Solid and so deceiving, locked away behind the dress shirt."

"I'm a fan of yours, too." He paused then asked, "Do you mind one more question?"

"What?" She stopped, not letting him go. Her eyes were still a little wet, but she stayed focused on him.

"You got away from him. What happened after that?"

"I got help for my addiction. Met an awesome guy who offered me an amazing job and who's now my boss, and I'm somewhat normal again. Oh, and therapy. Lots of therapy." She gave a half smile and tossed the napkin back on the table.

A fresh wave of guilt hit him. "Damn, Victoria. This is my fault, isn't it?"

She scoffed. "Yes, the perfect way to live life is blaming others for your own mistakes. No, Royce. I owned up to my errors a long time ago. I've paid my way for allowing rejection to drive bad decisions."

"Yes, but—"

"Save your buts and don't mention it again. There is no telling if the same mistakes would've happened or not. I've learned the here-and-now is what counts. I didn't think you'd be able to look at me without disgust once you found out."

She traced the contours of his chest and then grasped his hard cock through the fabric of his pants. "But you feel the exact opposite. You make me wet, Royce." When he groaned, she added, "If you want to be punished, I'll be happy to oblige you, but let's it make it for pleasure, not for any type of retribution."

"Yes. Whatever you want." The words tumbled out, his pulse pounding in his ears. He wanted to make her feel good, feel wonderful. To treat her like a queen as she deserved. A bit of retribution seemed required, no matter what she said. He'd strove to drag out the what-happened-between-then-and-now. Knowing how painful reliving those memories must've been, yet again made him feel obligated to let her have free rein for the remainder of their night together.

"Whatever I want? I'll hold you to that." She smiled and after a gentle squeeze to his package, moved away. "Go to the bed and bend over, shoulders to the mattress."

He obeyed. Centering on the mattress, he bent, head down, and linked his hands together above it when his shoulders were in position. A bag opened, the zipper rending like tearing paper. Then the snap of leather on flesh. His cock jerked. A low buzzing began in his ears. She intended to strike him. With a whip or crop or something else, he didn't know and didn't care. Another fantasy Victoria would fulfill for him. He'd kept his dream of being whipped to himself out of fear his ideas would be considered sick or depraved. Blindfolding, restraint with handcuffs, and being on the bottom were the public knowledge bits of his submissive musings. To tell someone he wanted to be hit, with anything, sent women running. He'd met plenty wanting to be flogged by him, but none desiring to service him the same way. *Until now.*

"Let those muscles loosen. Your back is clenched tight. Breathe. Relax," Victoria whispered in his ear. She nipped at the lobe then ran her tongue across the bite. Sting and soothe. "I said breathe."

Royce released a breath and took another slow one in. She landed the crop on his back in a playful pat. He loved it. His cock twitched as she love-tapped her way up and down his back, across his sides, preparing him for the true excitement.

"Are you ready, Royce?"

"Yes," he exhaled.

Chapter Four

It took a ton of control to keep from taking the stimulator she'd placed in her pocket and rubbing her clit with it. Instead, she hooked the waistband of his lounge pants and, with a gentle tug, slid them down to his knees.

Damn. His ass, toned, the peach skin in need of her mark, lay exposed.

She twirled the flogger. *Here goes nothing. Snap. Slap. Snap. Slap.* Both ass cheeks blushed at her. Royce's moan confirmed his pleasure.

"Do you want more?"

"Yes. Please...yes," he begged.

A new rush of arousal slicked her legs. How long could she keep going without seeking her own release? A few more strikes of the flogger and his sounds of pleasure filled the room. Victoria followed the moments of pain with a soothing rub of warm heat from her palm. Within minutes, she couldn't take it anymore. Leaning down, she bit his ass check.

"Oh, God," he moaned.

"Why, thank you. Get up." She tapped him on the shoulder and he got off the bed, his pupils dilated. Definitely, one hell of a night.

"What now?"

"Remove those pants and on all fours."

Royce raised an eyebrow and she expected him to refuse the instruction, but he followed her lead. Reaching into the pocket of the robe, she slipped the clit massager onto her index finger. Instead of using it on herself, she wanted to push him to the edge and then make him wait. She tapped his butt with the crop.

"Spread them, and I want you to grab your cock and masturbate for me."

He spread his legs farther apart and tugged on his cock. She turned on the clit massager and eased forward. Positioning the vibrating pink piece between his legs, she let it rest in the sensitive spot between his scrotum and his anus. He shuddered. "Have you ever had someone enter you here?"

"No," he groaned.

She continued massaging, his arousal increasing, hand

pumping up and down faster. "What do you want?"

"I want to...oh."

Victoria smiled. She loved how her presence and her finger could put him in such a state. "What?"

"I want to put my dick in you. Please."

"I won't make you beg. You want me. Take me."

Royce moved so fast she couldn't believe it, hauling her toward him. His lips crashed over hers, his kiss and custody ravenous. He caressed and maneuvered her to the bed at breakneck speed. Moisture trickled down her leg. She hadn't been so aroused in years.

He nipped at her lips and pushed her onto the mattress. Spreading the robe, she tugged it off. Not waiting for an invitation, he massaged her legs and spread them open, then traced his tongue along her thigh to ensure not a drop of her arousal would escape him.

He withdrew, his weight disappearing from the bed. Foil rustled. She opened her eyes and watched him slide latex in place. Then he braced his arms on either side of her body, stormy gaze locked on hers.

"May I?"

Such a simple question. She'd already given him permission. The fact that he asked again, his face strained and flush, revealed he barely held onto his control. The last vestiges of keeping sex and tonight casual fell away.

"Yes." Her turn to beg. "Please."

He lined his cock up with her entrance and she rubbed her clit against him, coating him in her arousal. Then Royce slammed into her again and again, in and out. Her body ran in stimulation overdrive, the need to orgasm spiraling tightly, ready to burst forth. She'd given him the opportunity to drive her insane.

"I'm—" Her voice cut off with a growl as he slowed his pace and took control.

"I'm sorry." He moaned, backing out of her until only the head of his cock still remained inside. "If I let you go over, I'll go, too. May I?"

Where he'd been trained she didn't know, hadn't asked. She'd expected him to be new to the whole experience, but he'd shown his training through his actions. He had knowledge of safewords and stayed conscious of asking permission even when in the throes of near-sexual release. She still had plenty to teach, but she'd planned on a sex night with a limited amount of dominance. Enough to give him pleasure and act out the fantasies he'd listed on his sheet. He'd certainly been acting out hers.

"Yes, hell yes."

He sighed, and began thrusting again. She massaged her nipples while he fingered her clit. The pressure points stimulated in tandem brought her to a crest and she saw stars, her pussy throbbing as the orgasm overtook her.

Her muscles clenched and pulsed around his cock, milking it for everything it held, refusing to let him escape. He'd never experienced an orgasm so intense before. Never thought it possible.

Victoria focused on him, and smirked, a fine sheen of sweat covering her skin. Nothing beat that moment, not one memory could replace it. He leaned down and gave her a kiss. She returned it, the sweet touch making him wonder how long before he'd be ready again. He'd be up for anything she wanted to do.

"Royce?" She snaked her arms around his midsection, dragging him to her.

"Yes?"

"I love you."

Royce let the last piece of anger fall away. Her emotions were anything but cold, not with him, and he wanted her. Always. "I love you, too, Tori."

Her eyes widened and he understood his error too late. She pushed against his chest and he withdrew from her. *Fuck.* Victoria flew off the bed, the bathroom door slamming before he could even formulate an acceptable response for his stupidity. One golden rule in a scene: never say the safeword unless he wanted things to stop. *I never should've chosen that one.*

After discarding the condom, he shoved his legs into his pants, needing to make things right. Fast. He knocked on the bathroom door. "Victoria. Please. Let me explain. I was caught up in the moment. I didn't mean to say the word. I didn't mean it like that."

A faucet turned off, a toilet flushed. Pressing his ear to the door, he listened for any sound to indicate her mood: items breaking, the sound of sniffles, or any movement.

The door flew open, an angry Victoria eyeing him. He jumped back. Jaw tight, eyes stormy, and her robe left open, she strode forward two steps. "Do you mean it?"

"Mean what?" Heat crawled up Royce's face. He had to stay focused even if she stood in front of him angry, naked, and sexy as hell.

"That you love me." The question in her eyes, the vulnerability, nearly broke him. She was afraid. Safeword be damned, that wasn't why she'd run.

"Yes. Of course I meant it!"

She crashed into him. In a wild frenzy, she smashed her lips to his. Their tongues battled for supremacy amidst roving hands and he wanted every bit of insanity, pain, or pleasure, she could give. Next stop—the bed.

Her eyes locked to his. "Then you better think of a new safeword."

Chapter Five

Sunlight streamed in through the window. Hard to believe she lay awake at eight o'clock in the morning. Mornings weren't her thing. Victoria stroked Royce's hair. His breaths were deep, a satisfied signal of perfectly peaceful sleep. She wished she could say the same. Instead butterflies swarmed in her gut.

She'd confessed her love and he'd returned it. Yet, how much could she trust that love? A man she'd once trusted with her heart had ripped her very existence from her. While she didn't doubt Royce would always protect her, she doubted his love matched hers. Did it encompass the possibility of a full relationship? Or at least dating to see where things would go?

Settling for being fuck buddies wasn't on her radar. She couldn't share Royce with anyone. Not after last night. Too many wonderful moments they'd shared prevented that. Incredibly hot moments, too. Surprisingly, they'd avoided catching the room on fire.

Speaking of that, she needed a glass of ice water. All that activity would dehydrate any libido.

She took her time dressing in a pair of panties, jeans, bra, and T-shirt. She needed a shower, but a quick trip to the ice machine didn't require full makeup and beauty regalia. After dumping out the puddle of water left in the ice bucket, she cast another glance at Royce, who softly snuffled into the pillow, and left. She'd need to order room service when she got back to the room. The idea of eating breakfast in bed sounded like the perfect start to their new beginning.

While she got ice, she daydreamed of how they might spend the rest of the day. Drive back to her place, a little heavy petting, order in pizza; things he may or may not want to do. Either way, she planned on giving him the option, the chance to continue beyond one night, in pursuit of a real relationship this time. Victoria smiled.

***

The ringing phone woke Royce. *Damn it.*
Clutching the receiver to his ear, he muttered, "Yes?"

"A friendly reminder that checkout is at eleven a.m. and thank you for staying at the Castillo Resort and Hotel of Fayetteville."

"Thank you." Royce hung up and swiped his eyes, a furtive effort to wipe away the remnants of sleep, coupled with a stretch of the arms and cursory flick of a finger to his morning woody. The night before had been amazing. Phenomenal. And, if everything went as he hoped, then maybe Victoria would be willing to discuss something a little more involved. Except...she'd disappeared.

He jumped from the bed. The bathroom door stood open, shower off, and every other piece of furniture remained person-less. A dull ache started in his gut. Mind racing, he thought of the previous night's activities. The words of love they'd exchanged, the snuggling after they'd been too exhausted to do anymore. *Now where the hell did she go?* Or had she made a run for it?

The door lock clicked before he could begin a search for her belongings. The sight of her walking through the door, all beautiful curvaceous body and gorgeous black hair, shot a flood of relief through him. His shoulders dropped. She'd returned with an ice bucket and appeared safe.

He dashed toward her. "You didn't leave."

"Leave? Why would I leave?" She chuckled and traced one side of his face.

"No reason." He shook his head. "Just fear. Stupid fear that you would want to run far away from last night."

She smiled and set the bucket on the floor. "I won't run from you. From this. In fact...." She began to nibble her lower lip in earnest.

"Yes? Don't be afraid, Victoria. Tell me what you want."

"You and me. Together after today. For movies and dinners, or a snuggle on the couch," she whispered.

She needed him, wanted him. He drew her into his arms and kissed her the way he should have eight years earlier, the way he'd kiss her every day if she let him. They were still as in tune as they'd been before. Probably more so. *Thank God.*

Leaning back, he gazed into her eyes. "I'll be whatever you need me to be."

What You Crave

Dedication

To my husband, for encouraging me to re-visit this world and giving me the initial idea for this story. I mutilated it a bit, but it's the thought that counts. 777

What You Crave

Sigmund Bermudez has spent the last year out of the BDSM scene, mourning the death of his father and rebuilding the family business. When he loses a bet to his bodyguard that Madame Eve won't locate a woman who's down with his type of kink, he finds himself committed to a date he's not sure he'll enjoy.

Lauren Elser has heard about kinky escapades from one of her more challenging patients, and never taken in part in one. When offered a chance to explore this undiscovered side of herself courtesy of 1Night Stand, she jumps at it.

Neither of them is prepared for the emotional rollercoaster that comes with their date, and soon shibari bondage play turns into so much more. The only problem, is Sig's not ready to open up and Lauren doesn't want to be used again. But if they work past the issues, there's a world of wonder in store.

Chapter One

Sigmund Bermudez read the email again, his fingers twisting a thin piece of nylon rope into an intricate knot. Another displeased Isle of Bermuda casino whale, and they wanted comp status.

"You need a night off."

Sig looked up from the email on his desk. "Nights off are for sorry sacks, who don't want to make money."

"Says my boss, whose casino makes more money than any other in the tri-state area." Kanoa, his bodyguard, said this with arms crossed, armband tattoos peeking out of the sleeves of his plain, black t-shirt. "Anyway, I'm not saying it because I believe it. This is a directive from upstairs."

Damn! His uncle was the cause of the email in front of him. Since Sig's father passed away they'd been in a constant struggle for power. The casino belonged to him, not his father's brother, who cared more for living a decadent lifestyle than managing the million-dollar business on the verge of pulling out of the red. "He's not the most reliable person to give advice. Especially since he offended one of our biggest whales."

"Sir?"

"Don't go there. You've never called me 'Sir'. Don't start now." They'd known each other too long for formalities, serving together in the military, while bonding over MRE's and cold night patrols. They reserved 'Sir' for high-ranking officers and he didn't constitute as one.

"An attempt at respect because you won't like what I have to say."

"I may not like it, but don't try to placate me. Spit it out." His fingers continued twisting and looping the ends of the rope through the rings of the emerging design.

Kanoa stepped up to the desk and placed both palms flat against the dark cherry wood, the tribal sleeve on his arm a foreboding reminder that his friend enjoyed pain like Sig enjoyed ropes. "You're working too hard, too much, and setting yourself up for failure."

Both eyebrows went up. "Really? Last time I checked we were

making a profit again."

"Yes, but your patrons and employees aren't happy with the person running things. I've heard talk you're too uptight and far too quick to alienate yourself from everyone. Speaking of, when did you last play a scene?"

He straightened up in his chair, tucking the finished rope square into his pocket. "None of your business." The last time he'd bothered to indulge his kind of fantasies, sexual or dominant, had been before his father's death.

"I'm your friend and bodyguard, it's my business."

"A year."

"Hell." Kanoa swung away from the desk and marched over to the massive window overlooking the main casino floor. The t-shirt and blue jeans look made a stark contrast to his own three-piece suit. "To remain celibate in a war zone is one thing. Self-induced deprivation is crap when you've got a whole room full of women ripe for the picking."

"I don't want a woman who's damaged or suffering from an addiction. Not to mention most of them wouldn't know what a scene is."

His friend scoffed. "They're not all like that and a good portion don't know what they are missing."

"There's not enough time in my schedule to waste trying to find out." The fact remained his particular tastes were hard to satisfy. Most women wanted a man who'd give them safe, vanilla sex with maybe a few rough moments involving pulled hair or driving them against a wall. He wanted more than those basic, simplistic ideas of sensuality... he craved his partner's submission and obedience. "And you know how I like my women. I'm not going to find one out there."

"But what if you could?"

"What the hell are you talking about?" If he had a nickel for every time Kanoa spoke in riddles he wouldn't need to work so hard to save his family's business.

"How about a bet? If I can find a woman interested in your type of fun, would you agree to a date and whatever else follows, without complaint?"

"Do you want to lose a bet to me again?"

His bodyguard was no gambler. No, the man fared better in picking up women or fighting assholes. "I've got the winning hand this time. I know the perfect service to find what you're looking for."

"Don't tell me about it. Just do whatever you're going to do. At least you asked me before you did it."

"How do you know?" Kanoa smiled, leaving the room.

Back to work. Sig picked up his phone ready to make an apologetic call and crossed his fingers, hoping to keep another whale from diving overboard.

***

"I don't think this is a good idea." Lauren Elser pushed the card across her glass top coffee table.

Victoria, a practicing Dominant and the patient on her couch, lifted her head. "Wasn't it you who told me to embrace my inner cravings? To free my desires from the crushing weight of my past relationships?"

"Yes, I said something along those lines but..."—how to put this tactfully—"I'm your therapist and it's not ethical for me to talk about this with you."

"We talk about everything else." Victoria moved to a sitting position. "In fact, I've told you things I don't tell anyone else."

Her patient spoke the truth, but infatuations with a person's sexual practices were inappropriate. Yet each appointment they spent a good chunk of time having 'healthy' conversations about preferred fetishes, sexual encounters with other submissives, and any current adventures the Domme had with her boyfriend. Through all their talks it'd been difficult to not profess a curiosity in the lifestyle or admiration for the uncharted experimentation the empowered woman willingly engaged in.

She'd spent as much time analyzing her own thoughts and found herself most aroused by dominant practices. Relinquishing control to someone and in return being granted pleasure appealed to her on many levels. She indulged in the fantasy of what such an encounter would detail, talking about limits and locating hers, but the lines had blurred.

"I'm not trying to convince you," the Domme said. "You don't have to discuss your preferences either. It's just a card. A card I'm going to leave here. You can go to the website or not. It's an option and I won't break any of your rules, either."

The timer buzzed, a blessing and a curse. Lauren opened her mouth to speak, but before she did—

"Well, I guess that's it for today. I'll tell Royce you said hello. See you next week." Victoria stood and bolted out the door, for safety purposes, no doubt. Lauren glanced at the card, with Madame Eve's 1Night Stand Service embossed in gold on a black background.

She stuffed the rectangle temptation into her suit pocket to get it off the table before her next client came in.

***

Two hours later her client appointments were done for the day and the damn card burned a hole in her pocket; like a magic talisman from some fantasy movie calling out to her. She'd been trying so hard to forget about it, attempting to occupy herself with updating patient files and cataloging her notes. Then it evolved into rocking side-to-side in her chair, until she gave in and pulled the card out. What harm came from visiting the site? turned into What harm came from filling out an application? and then she fell down the rabbit hole.

There were preferences - very detailed preferences - to fill out. The final check box involved acknowledging a disclaimer about matches not being instantaneous or in some cases not found at all. Madame Eve took her job seriously.

Much more than her ex, Randall, whose idea of pleasure involved a race to get off as fast as possible with very little effort on his end. She topped, she blew and jacked him and he rarely returned the favor. He'd tended to her orgasms in the early stages of their relationship, the magic time when a man would do anything to please his woman, to secure a spot in her life. After those courting rituals were over and his role assured, the asshole revealed his true colors. Too bad she'd wasted more than a year on such a worthless cause.

Lauren went through each field twice, listing out favorite foods, beverages, scents, colors, and then it took a turn toward her sexual inclinations. She expressed her interest in submission, but indicated she had no clue about her limits. By the time she'd uploaded a picture and pressed submit the sun had already set in the Fall sky. With no more time to waste, she shut things down and headed out the door.

Chapter Two

The Castillo Hotel of Fayetteville had swanky accommodations, but they didn't hold a candle to his honeymoon suites at Isle of Bermuda. Still, Sig was happy his date would occur here and not at his own casino and hotel. Less chance of being recognized, and if things didn't work out then all the easier for him to sneak out without notice.

Hell, thanks to Kanoa, he had no reason to be worried. He booked the room under an assumed name, the one he used for his application on Madame Eve's site. Tonight, his name was John.

He couldn't believe this dating site found him someone interested in bondage. At the BDSM clubs he used to frequent, women or men interested in the type of play he enjoyed were few and far between. Most of his encounters were spent with sub's who wanted to 'experiment', and then backed out before things got too involved, with ropes or with him.

"I've swept each room. Everything appears clean," his bodyguard announced, entering the main living area of the suite.

To keep things private he'd purchased the largest room they had, equipped with living area, dining area, bedroom and bathroom. She had the option to leave whenever she wanted. He'd be surprised if they made it past dinner. If she chickened out, which seemed likely, then the night ended with him alone, dessert and maybe a movie on television.

Still, he'd arrived prepared. Hoisting his duffel bag onto his shoulder he headed for the bedroom. "Then I'll start setting things up."

The four-poster bed and white bedding were perfect. A small part of him hoped the gorgeous woman wanted to take things further than a simple scene. To spread her out across the comforter and tie her up would please him just fine, though. Multiple scenarios had rattled around in his brain since he'd been granted access to her photo and her basic likes and dislikes.

He strode over to the black, low-sitting dresser and opened his bag. Gathering the rope chains he set them out, organizing them and taking pleasure in reviewing the varying varieties, colors, and lengths. Nylon cording, his preference for new sessions, made up the bulk of the collection. Nylon held shape better, stood up to multiple types of knots, and worked well on bondage virgins. Yet, he kept a few cords of silk on hand, with small diameters designed for tiny jobs— ideally, nipples. The hemp and jute he'd left at the office.

"Think you've got enough rope?" Kanoa stood beside him, eyes wide. His finger moved through the air counting the number of chains on the dresser top.

Sig placed a knife, scissors, lighter, and candles out beside them. "It pays to be prepared."

"Really? Then what the hell is this other stuff for?"

"Finding out would require showing me more of yourself than you want to." He didn't discriminate when it came to bondage, though sexually he preferred women. Tying someone up aroused him, speaking to the side of him that liked control. Gender didn't matter in those moments, submission did.

"You're right." His bodyguard rubbed one of the ropes, sliding his fingers up and down the chain. "Sometimes I wonder.... Do you need anything else?"

"You to get the hell out of here before she arrives." His friend didn't look like a hotel employee and in many cases his bulky frame intimidated people he wanted to impress. He refused to take chances and freak his date out.

Kanoa frowned. "Fine. I'll be across the hall if you need me."

"I won't." He'd protested the original plan with them booking adjoining rooms, separating them by a single door. No sense in rousing his bodyguard's protective side if things got heated or loud. He enjoyed a little noise from his subs during the act and liked to hear them cry out his name.

"You're still sore about losing the bet aren't you?"

He shrugged. "Maybe I'm more worried she'll be like Ashlynn."

"Nope, Ashlynn wins the award for most awful woman. She wound you up so tight, then cheated on you and had the nerve to call you depraved."

"She's into cuckolding." Too bad he believed in monogamy.

"Sure, everyone's got their fetishes, but you talk about them. Not hide them in dark until you can't control yourself."

"She knew what she was doing." Thank goodness the one time she'd decided to bring another man to their bed turned out to be the night she'd broken things off. The unfortunate part is it happened hours before his father died. He still hadn't determined if her little stunt helped him or hurt him, but since then dating had been out of the question.

"Promise you'll give this one a chance?"

He held his hands up and took a step back from the dresser. "It's all up to her. I'll be my usual charming self, but if she's not into me or the scene, it won't be my fault."

No sense in admitting he looked forward to the encounter with each passing moment or mentioning that he planned to truly give this woman a chance.

***

Damn. Nervous energy had Lauren's arms and legs shaking in some strange dance as she stood in front of the hotel room door. She'd read the information Madame Eve sent her half a dozen times over the last week and jumped up and down in joy when the date night details were emailed to her. The turtleneck sweater dress, panty hose, and black suede ankle boots seemed too prim for a rendezvous at a swanky hotel, but the chilly weather had her choosing comfort and warmth over sexy. Besides, scenes weren't sex.

She knocked, a couple light taps. Maybe he'd changed his mind. A lie since she'd already checked with the front desk.

The barrier swung open and the picture became a reality. Hell, the picture didn't do him justice. A two-piece pinstripe suit, black hair long enough to run her fingers through, and russet brown eyes taking her in from head to toe...scrumptious.

"Lauren?" Her name came out pure and sensual when spoken with a perfect rolling 'r'.

A large lump took up residence next to her vocal cords and she responded with a nod. She'd always been more of a listener than a talker.

"Would you like to come in?" He stepped back making a path for her. Beyond the entrance the room sat bathed in shadows and orange light from a lit fireplace, beckoning to her.

She swallowed and then cleared her throat. "Yes."

Walking forward she caught a hint of his smell, cedar and citrus, similar to her favorite candles she kept throughout her apartment.

"Let me take your coat, and then I'll get you a glass of water. The air's dry."

So, he'd noticed her scratchy voice. Check the box next to attentive, and another check for downright sexy. He stopped behind her, pausing for a moment before grasping the edges of her coat. His fingers brushed her shoulders and the warmth seeped through the wool and cotton blend of her dress. "Did you find the place all right?"

Her arms slipped out of the sleeves and she took a few steps forward, the trench coat dragging away from her body. "Yes. I've read about the hotel, but never had the pleasure to stay here."

"Well, I'm happy to give you a chance at a new experience."

A double entendre? "Do you stay here often?"

His information mentioned no relationships in over a year, but sexual encounters didn't require a lasting commitment.

"No, it's my first time here also." He draped her coat over an armchair then stood in front of a small bar against the wall, pouring bottled water over ice.

He approached with slow steps, a smile emerging on his face, and extended the glass toward her. "You don't talk much. Are you shy, or do I frighten you?"

"I'm not much for talking." Her words came out soft, mirroring his tone. Maybe he expected her to be afraid. "Are women generally scared when they meet you?"

"They're a bit timid, but not because of me. My ropes shock them."

"Then show them to me."

"Follow me." He turned and headed for the bedroom.

She gripped the glass tight, took a sip, and then exhaled after swallowing. Where she'd gotten the nerve to be brazen surprised her, but no time to change her mind now. She straightened her back and followed him into the room. He flipped the light switch and two white lamps flickered on. He motioned to the dresser and she took a good look. At least eight different rope chains were laid out on top. All of them with varying lengths and diameters, and the colors ranged from red to purple, the colors of the rainbow.

"You're interested in submissive rope play, or as some call it, shibari?" He was so forthright with this question, like he expected it to scare her away. Instead she wanted to get closer, respecting his choice to keep everything black and white. No blurry gray lines. No false pretenses.

"Yes."

"Then let's get started." He moved forward.

She instinctively put her arms out. "What? But... I don't know anything about you."

"The info sheet Madame Eve provided didn't tell you anything?" One eyebrow lifted in question. He shrugged out of his suit coat and hung it in the closet.

"Uh..." Rational thought fled as his meticulous, manicured fingers rolled up the sleeves of his shirt, revealing tanned skin and a smattering of dark arm hair. Did it cover his chest? "Those were basic facts. What about family, relationships, expectations?"

He tugged at the bottom of his shirt now, untucking it from the waistband and she caught a flash of a silver belt buckle. "Tell me all those things."

She didn't swoon when he slid his shoes off and sat in the chair to remove his socks. John being naked during the scene was listed in the info as well and played havoc with her intentions to stay focused. "I live alone. Parents are alive. No siblings. No long-term relationships and very few dates."

"Because..." He sat there, barefoot, one corner of his mouth upturned in a semi-mocking smile.

"Because I like to eat and converse before I take my clothes off with anyone."

"Touché." He pushed out of the chair and strutted over to her. "How do you feel about surf and turf?"

"I'm not a lobster fan."

He leaned in, hot breath fanning her ear. "I believe I can change your mind."

"Lead and I'll follow."

He chuckled. "Those are the perfect words."

***

Sig had expected to put fear in her eyes with the ropes, but instead he found interest. When he prodded, she stood firm, unflappable and more than willing to match his every move. She passed his test with flying colors. So, he dined with her. Succulent mesquite smoked lobster, tender filet mignon, steamed vegetable medley and a complement of wines, two whites and one red. She mirrored his suggestions without question. He wished her turtleneck to perdition, the better to view the fine lines of her neck when sipped from the glass as instructed. How would his rope look tied around her in a leash?

How fast she'd ensnared him with a shy smile and her quiet demeanor. He liked her simple, understated style, her bundled dark blonde hair, and the single silver chain with a cross.

"Is that a Celtic knot?" He asked after taking a sip of Pinot Grigio to wash way the last remnants of his lobster.

"Why, yes." She reached up and pressed the metal between two fingers. "I saw it in a gift shop and had to have it."

"Really?"

She grinned, spinning the cross, the motion much like rope

twisting beneath his fingers. "Really. Did you have some other picture in mind?"

"Maybe a family heirloom or a gift from the last short-lived love affair?"

Her back went straight before she lifted her arms from the table and leaned back into the chair. Until now, conversation had been innocuous and surface scratching. They'd discussed interests in food and found similarities in tastes and style preferences in furniture, with a brief mention of the suite decorations included. He'd kept the topics safe, but he wanted to nudge again. Wanted the rush he experienced before when she didn't back down.

"My relationships didn't ever last long enough for gifts."

"Because..." He waited, and as usual his hands sought their own occupation, twisting the cloth napkin into a simple slipknot.

"I had career goals. Relationships were a natural casualty in my pursuit of professional success. The one guy I got serious about—" She smothered a laugh with her palm.

He understood. "It's weird wanting to tell someone you just met anything and everything."

"You have no idea. I'm not used to doing the talking."

Her job, a therapist. He'd been recommended to one, but preferred to work through his leftover emotions by saving the casino. Words were not action. Still, a profession like hers no doubt came with a big emotional cost. "I'm told doctors need therapy too. Keep going."

Instead of rebuking at his gentle command, she relaxed. Tension eased from her shoulders, arms going to the armrests on the dining room chair. "His name isn't worth mentioning, but he didn't cut it... in the sack."

"Too vanilla?"

"Too concerned with his own orgasm, and any requests or lack of enthusiasm earned me some rude responses. Then he told me I'm too frigid to try new sexual experiences. So I got rid of him."

"Ouch." Sig stood, walked around the table, and offered to help her up. She took it. "I'll try to make sure I meet all your needs, then."

She laughed, a throaty, melodic sound, which had his half-mast cock springing to full attention. "I'd like a good submissive experience to see if this is something I want."

"Are you enjoying yourself?" Time to find out if she'd admit to her submissiveness from the moment she'd walked in the door. He directed her actions and so far she'd capitulated like a pro.

"Yes."

"What do you want?" Normally he'd never ask such a question.

It laid the foundation for a sub to top from the bottom, which he'd never agree to or condone.

"I want your ropes."

ChapterThree

Lauren was thankful for wearing dark clothing because her panties were more than damp. His voice and commands should have appalled her and unleashed the inner feminist. Instead, the exact opposite occurred: A primal need took over to allow him to direct her, to relinquish the reins and enjoy the journey. And if his mouth proved an equal physical talent to his ability with words, the date would be worth it.

Not to mention she found herself blurting out the strangest things, and answering questions about herself she didn't discuss with friends. John, whose name didn't fit him, inspired brutal honesty. She wanted their interactions to occur without artifice. At some point during dinner she'd decided to move forward with the scene and with him standing next to her, she started to want more than just bondage.

His questioning expression turned feral, eyes darkening in lust, lips pursing into a triumphant sneer. On anyone else she'd believe them to be arrogant. On him it looked empowering. In a fast second the grin turned into a serious, focused stare. "Then take the dress off."

A challenge. He liked to challenge, to set limits and see if she'd surpass them. Similar to her clients' lines in the sand, she'd cross every barrier, break every wall. She reached for the belt around her waist and unsnapped the clasps. It thumped against the floor. The hem of her dress bunched in her hands and she wished he'd do this. She longed for him to touch her.

Instead, he watched. The bulge in his pants grew more pronounced when she dragged the black fabric up her thighs and over her stomach to reveal the garters securing her thigh highs to boy shorts. He whistled low and she tugged the thick dress over her head. The challenge came in removing the rest of the garment artfully, which proved near impossible with arms stretched above her.

"Do you need help?" A question he didn't allow her to answer. His warm palms flattened along her sides, sliding up around her breasts. Several calluses brushed against her skin and inspired a shiver, which arced through her. He grabbed the fabric from her and plucked it clear, tossing it onto the dinner chair.

The warmth of him disappeared as he stepped away from her. "Do you always dress this sexy under your therapist clothes?"

Her choice of black lace on black lace with the sheer hose had been spur of the moment. Rarely did she dress in a similar fashion in the office, although sometimes... "Not for the workplace, but at home I'll dress up like this and parade in front of the mirror."

"You like watching yourself."

"I guess."

He crooked a finger, beckoning her, and she went, suckered in by the desire to have his hands on her again. "Interesting." He linked her fingers with his and maneuvered her toward the bedroom. "Before we get started let me tell you how things will work. I'm a masochist. I get off by prolonging my release. The longer I have to wait the better. So for this first part, I'm going to explore your body with the ropes and it will take time."

"What about sex?"

"Not what our evening is about, and scenes are so much more." They reached the room and he backed her up to the bed, ending the link between them. "Since this is your first time let's go over the rules. No talking without my permission. The word pink will get me to stop. Say red and I cut any ropes, no hesitation. All right?"

She nodded.

"Lay down on the bed."

Following his command, she sighed, the surface of the comforter cooled her heated body and the pillows sunk beneath her weight.

John turned, one of the ropes draped across his shoulder. "Some people are afraid to submit because they fear not knowing. Since this is your first time I'll make you a deal."

When he reached the bed, he slid two fingers down the inside of her calf until both encircled her ankle right above her boot top.

Shivering, she spoke, unable to keep the question back. "What's the deal?"

"For every command you follow, I'll tell you what I plan to do next. Do you agree?"

She swallowed, her throat tight and the air heavy with the promise in his words. Her only way to respond—a single nod.

"I need a yes."

"Yes," she croaked, before letting her elbows give way and her shoulders hit the mattress.

"Spread your legs."

She opened them wide, determined to outperform his

expectations.

He chuckled. "You're limber, I like that in a submissive. I'm going to bind each ankle in a simple two-column tie to the two posts of this bed. Here and here." He pointed to each post and then did as promised, crafting exquisite knots around the ankles of her boots. Looped and wrapped around the toe and the heel, the ropes extended her instep.

Once both were complete he asked her, "Are they too tight?"

Laura shook her head. The binding appeared more like extensions of her shoes.

Hands slid up her leg and she'd wished her stockings would disappear. The absence of skin-to-skin contact proved an agony, but no doubt part of his arousal and another way to deprive himself. "Spread your arms wide."

No hardship there. The natural progression would be to secure her arms and she craved it. Wanted him to pick up the pace, to explore and give her more than he promised.

Grabbing another coil, he moved onto the wrists. Those talented fingers were coarse and rough on her skin, but the simple touches intensified her desire. Instead of being cold, the room temperature rose and he'd done nothing more than tie up her limbs.

"I'll finish with a shibari cuff, or as some refer to it, a boola-boola knot," his words were whispered and a fingernail scraped the sensitive flesh near the veins on her wrist.

She hissed.

"Did I hurt you?"

A quick shake, no.

"You can talk. In fact, tell me how you feel."

The wide smile she displayed surprised her.

"I didn't know I was being humorous." He massaged the skin he'd marked and winked.

"It's not every day someone wants to know my feelings. I'm the one asking those types of questions." No, people dumped on her. In some cases, it took months of sessions to start the patient talking and through all of it no one cared how she felt. They weren't supposed to.

The wrapping of the rope continued, and he spoke while continuing to symmetrically cover her wrist. "I promise it won't be painful."

"Anxious. I want to tug, to squirm."

"Why?"

She glanced at the three-looped black rope around her wrist. John tucked and tugged on the last tie. "Because I'm aroused."

"It's natural to become aroused during this type of play. All my scenes are intimate, but deprivation is the most gratifying experience. Driving myself to the brink of release, watching the skin abrade from the ropes. Knowing my voice, the binding, and a single touch will make you writhe is more exhilarating than release. Trust me."

His words were pure reverence to the craft and she wanted to find the place, the headspace, which allowed her to let go. "I trust you."

"Then I'm going to blindfold you."

***

He expected fear to immediately take hold. Blindfolding tended to cause debate from a bottom. Instead, Lauren, spread-eagled and skin blushing, nodded her agreement.

His cock never came down since the moment her dress came off, but like he told her the longer he had to wait, the better. Yet, he'd promised her this wasn't about sex. To take it to a deeper level without her permission... hell, to ask for permission, he'd be pushing the boundaries too far. Better to keep going, give her a pretty rope corset and let it inspire her. From there he planned on changing her ankle and wrist ties into a harness, or maybe a cage. There were so many options and not enough hours to do everything he wanted to her body.

He gathered a slip of black fabric from the dresser and sat next to her on the bed. She trembled.

"Close your eyes, Lauren." Stretching the elastic band, he slid the blindfold in place. "Now let yourself feel. Get lost in the way the lines rub against you."

Nylon scratched the skin, not harsh like hemp or cotton, but enough so the sub's skin would abrade. Already the tone of her flesh near the bound wrists had turned a dark pink.

"Does anything feel numb or cold?"

"No," she responded, head arched back, the thin column of her neck exposed. A leash needed to adorn it. He'd make sure it did.

"I'm going to wrap you in a rope corset. It will go underneath your breasts and below the waist."

Sig grabbed the blue skein. Once unraveled, he made a loop in the middle of the rope, holding it right below the waist with two fingers. Lauren's breath turned shallow and he didn't miss the little spark zipping through him when any piece of his skin brushed hers. He moved forward, choosing to ignore his aching cock, and focus on drawing the tied ends through the bight.

Then she moaned. "I'm hot."

"It's not nice to brag." He made another pass around her body and another tuck through the opening, completing the Lark's Head. She kept squirming, jutting her breasts out by arching off the bed, and he positioned his arm just so the pointed tips of her nipples brushed against it. Torture so exquisite, yet the sharp huffs of breath she let loose didn't make him move faster.

What would her breasts look like without the bra? Pale flesh with dark nipples? Or soft and creamy? Each rotation around her body, each encounter with the lace bra ratcheted his interest, until he had to unwind the corset. He needed her exposed to complete a more arousing bondage pose. "May I remove your bra?"

Her throat bobbed on a swallow. His cock rebelled, throbbing in his pants at her pink lips parting. "Please. Undo the clips securing the straps."

The clasps at the back went first, and in his haste he found the problem. Bound wrists prevented the removal of any fabric. He searched and found the clips she'd mentioned. Once undone the bra could be whisked away, except he did it slowly, allowing the lace to scrape against her nipples.

She thrashed and groaned.

"I won't touch you again until you stop." The warning worked. All movement halted. The room went quiet. The only sound— her breathing. And he did his best to control his.

"How do you feel now?" Starting over, this time he formed a bight above the breasts, circling it around her body, sliding the ends through the opening and cinching the closure tight against her back.

"I want more."

"Don't be vague. More rope?" He smiled while forming the first 'L' shape in the front, her breasts secured between four lines of nylon above and below, a shinju. Her nipples were like twin cherries, larger than what he was accustomed to, and they called to him. Erect and firm. "I'm going to touch you now." He tweaked one of them with a forefinger and thumb.

Her growl made him want to reach for the other one, but he held off.

"A pair of dark, red pearls. Perfect." He straddled her now, moving his mouth down to engulf one of the pearls while he completed the same knotting system at her back, the final piece to the harness. Once done he moved away, letting go of the flesh he teased between his teeth.

"I'm going to remove the blindfold. When I do look to your left."

Tugging the fabric off her eyes, she turned her head and gasped. "Good?"

***

She couldn't believe it. Her panties had remained damp from the moment he began fondling her body. Now, they were soaked. With her limbs tied, her chest wrapped in blue nylon... the sight of those ropes did something to her insides, and she bucked upward. "Yes. Now your hands."

She wanted his tanned skin against her pale white. Those fingers and palms back on the pearls he'd complimented moments before.

Her limited verbal plea worked because his palms brushed over both peaks. A moan escaped her and she cried, "Please."

His head came low then, the visual blocked by his hair, but she felt everything. Hot mouth replacing skin, teeth grazing. The seconds dragged on with the administered torture and pleasure to not one, but both of her nipples. Then he whispered, "Do you want me to touch other places?"

She nodded, and a feral smile replaced his neutral expression.

Hot, callused skin connected with hers, sliding down her stomach, past her waist, and heading for the juncture between her thighs. More adventures led her to waxing earlier in the day, and she had a perfect landing strip, trimmed for this occasion. Not that she'd planned on this, but she'd hoped.

"I don't normally do this." One hand slipped between lace and flesh.

She shivered. "Then I'm the lucky one."

A single digit glided over her clitoris and flicked the nub. Panting became her natural state like a dog, and she didn't dare move for fear he'd stop. Another finger joined the fray, tracing the outside of her labia minora— holy hell! She'd reverted to high school biology terms. The slow movements, the careful exploration, made her crazy. The urge to scream, to cry out for penetration sat so close to the surface and the best way to stow the impulse involved reviewing what he did to her, how he did it.

Finally, he plunged both fingers inside at once and she let out a cry, some insane mewling noise. Her orgasm grew closer. Closer than she expected, but John had been right— delayed gratification increased the satisfaction.

He moved quickly, pumping in and out while tweaking her nipples. The pressure rose, a coiling sensation in her lower back and abdomen preceding the coming eruption, like a balloon ready to explode. She tugged at her bindings, straining against them and loving the burn, the pain they left while the peak rose higher.

As she crested, she called out "John!"

"No," he said, his voice guttural and rough. "Call me Sig."

Before she could ask what the hell? her release rushed forth, her legs jolting against the ties and moisture coating the fingers inside her. Eyesight blurred momentarily, the force stronger than ever before but all too soon reality came seeping back in. The name in her mind, the name she'd called, wasn't real? "Who's Sig?"

"I am." He stared her straight in the eyes. The words were true and she felt exposed, manipulated, and embarrassed.

"Red."

Chapter Four

Fear gripped him, but he sliced through the bindings regardless. Some Doms cared more about the rope, but in his mind things mattered less than people did. With the last of the color cordage discarded, he helped her to a standing position. "Are you all right?"

Her balance appeared unsteady as she bent to pick up her bra, and she regained it with a hand against the wall. "Where's the bathroom?"

"Right through there." He pointed toward a doorway set near the closet and stepped back to let her pass, gripped with an urge to offer assistance, but he fought against it.

The ruined date left him with a mass of guilt and a rather painful erection. Just what he deserved. When she'd called out his fake name, the one on the hotel registry books, the one designed to give him anonymity for the evening, it worked against him. When she said "John" he'd spoken without thought. He wanted her to cry out his name. To be his, not some fake persona's. Her reaction to the bondage stunned him. She enjoyed seeing herself restrained or she'd been too far gone, lost in some agonizing state of arousal, to want to stop— begging for connection, for release. Words weren't needed for him to discern what she craved. His instincts about her needs were triggered the moment she walked in the door. A strange connection and now he'd wrecked it.

When she came out of the bathroom, bra and panties in place, skin still pink around her wrists and the indentations from the pearl harness still present, he had the urge to tie her up all over again. This time though, the idea of having her envelope his cock, not his fingers, came to mind. First things first. "I'm sorry."

"Who the hell are you?" Hair pulled back into a simple ponytail and a frown told him the post-orgasm glow had been washed away.

"My name is Sigmund Bermudez. Friends call me Sig."

Shaking his hand in a firm grip, she replied, "Lauren Elser. Let's try this again, shall we?"

The physical connection sent a buzz of lust zinging through his body. Once they extinguished the shake, she stalked out of the bedroom. He followed. Thank goodness he'd kept most of his clothes on.

She'd already tugged the dress over her head and into place, and stood at the small bar along the wall pouring herself a glass of water. "Thirsty?"

The atmosphere changed, as if he no longer held control and instead signed up for examination by microscope. "I can get my own drink." A snappy response, sure, but he didn't like ceding control. Ever.

"Fine. Would you mind telling me what you do for living?"

"I own a business."

"The notes I received said as much." She took a sip of water. "But again, it said your name is John and you've told me otherwise. So I have to ask, because I need to know what else you're lying about."

He grabbed a glass and dropped some ice cubes and a splash of whiskey into it. A quick throwback and his throat burned. The sting of the alcohol would give him the courage to come clean.

"Wait... Bermudez? As in Isle of Bermuda Hotel and Casino?"

At least Madame Eve had selected a woman with a brain. In fact, he admired her intelligence along with her body. No sense in denying it. "I'm the CEO as of last October."

She glanced up at the ceiling, shaking her head. "Wow. A year as CEO and now you have the sudden interest in a date? I'm sure you get plenty of girls."

"How about we sit down?" He motioned toward the couches, choosing to take one and hoping she'd take the other. She did, crossing her legs. Those legs. Hell, he wished they were wrapped around him instead of closed off.

Lauren cleared her throat and he stopped staring.

"I guess you could say I don't have time to date or find someone who'd be interested in my type of activities. The whole application on Madame Eve's site happened because I lost a bet." Being honest sucked, more so when she rolled her eyes.

"A bet sounds a little far-fetched."

"Believe what you want, but when I saw Madame Eve's description of you I became interested in learning more. Meeting you tonight has been the highlight of my whole year, beyond getting my casino out of the red. I've enjoyed our time together, but I understand if you want to leave. Lying is something I don't agree with. Yet..."

Confessions were good for the soul right? Talking about the past and clearing the air, territory he'd steered clear of until now.

"Go on." She prodded, setting her glass on the coffee table

separating them.

"I'm familiar with the pain falsehoods can cause. My ex told me she got off on my kind of kink. She fell in line with it, pandering to every whim and rope idea I had. Feelings got involved, and then when I was ready to offer her more she brought another man into our bed before confessing to despising bondage." Old anger and memories drifted to the surface. One reason he didn't talk about it in detail.

"I'm sorry. Does it make you angry?"

Sig ground his teeth. "A little. She screwed me over. Your ex did the same thing, right? Drew you in, made you care, and then told you you weren't good enough."

"I can say I'm still sore about how things played out, but I try to look at the situation from a positive side too. If it wasn't for my ex I'd have never filled out an application on Madame Eve's site and I'd still be at home instead of in this amazing hotel with you."

He glanced up. The smile on her face held him sway, along with the genuine honesty he found in her gaze. Regardless of his lies, she appeared to still be happy with the evening... happy with him. "Even though I lied to you."

The light in her eyes dulled. "I'll admit I'm still a bit frustrated that you hid yourself from me. Not the best way to go about this. I make it a habit to know who I'm allowing access to my body. And I feel like you took advantage of my honest nature."

He rose from the couch, circumvented the table, and pointed to the cushion next to hers. "May I?"

She nodded.

Sitting next to her he breathed in her scent, apples and cinnamon, Fall personified. How to make her understand? Did he want to let her in so deep? "Everything, except for the name and keeping my career to myself, is me. The bondage, the wine tasting, football-loving and ex-military life is me. Hiding my name and career is just part of -"

"Keeping yourself from being hurt."

Damn. She called him out without provocation. Then she sunk in for the kill, and boy, did the verbal blade hurt.

"I'm not in high school nor am I some early twenties drama queen who surrounds herself with people playing make-believe games. I walked through the door tonight expecting someone to be real with me, to show me adventure, and keep things honest."

No one ever set him down in such a way, except for his mother. She'd been gone a lot longer than his father, but taught him to stay grounded. "I'm sorry. Deeply sorry, and I want to make it up to you."

"How?" Her turn to challenge. Those blue eyes still simmered with anger, and with something else as well. If he read her right, it would all work out.

"Sneak out with me. Let me show you who I am."

She thinned her lips, the action equal parts adorable and teasing. Her foot waved in the air, some nervous tic and he loved making her nervous. She whispered, "Yes," pairing her verbal agreement with a single nod.

"All right, take my hand," he said, standing up.

She linked her palm in his and he tugged her off the couch.

"Let's go."

***

Lauren didn't know where Sig planned on taking her. She should've asked, but stopped short, afraid to break the magic of the moment or his courage. Sneaking down the hallway to the elevator brought out memories of the teenage girl from yesteryear who tiptoed to avoid squeaks in the floor when she escaped to late-night parties. When the elevator doors shut, she giggled.

"What?" He grinned.

"This secret agent aspect of getting out of here reminds me of my younger days. But why are we creeping down the halls?"

The grin disappeared. "My job and the hazards involved mean I have a bodyguard following me around all the time. For once I want to do something without him knowing about it. To be able to show you what I am minus the part of who I am."

"Where are we going?" She loved how he kept their connection and refused to let go of her hand. How he squeezed it before he spoke, as if re-establishing how they were together in this.

"Where I spend most of my time... Isle of Bermuda."

All right. He planned to show her things and she'd driven him to an edge. Hell, she'd expected him to kick her out or agree to the night being over. Instead he broke down a wall, one she hadn't noticed until he told her his real name. Then the signs appeared larger than an elephant. Caught up in the moment she'd put aside her job instincts at the beginning of the evening and believed she could relax without analyzing. After the truth about his name those ingrained therapist parts came back involuntarily, but her emotions were already involved and with someone who didn't have room for another person within their crap-to-deal-with sphere.

His car turned out to be some fancy thing, black, sleek, and with plenty of power. She shrunk into the passenger seat and ran her fingers across the leather details. Surrounded by such luxury dropped her mood into a place of inferiority, until he reached over, caressing her with his fingertips and forging a connection between them once more.

"Thank you."

"For?"

"For encouraging me to talk. I can say I've felt more alive since you walked into the hotel room tonight than I have in over a year."

Those words sparked a flash of hope like the initial spark in a light bulb. Such a statement fed the part of her searching and clawing to be more adventurous. The sentence implied she'd inspired him the entire evening, and encompassed the insanity-inducing moments when she'd been at the mercy of his ropes and his clever fingers.

"How are we going to avoid attention when we get to your casino?"

He smiled. "A secret entrance. My father had it commissioned when the plans were first drawn. He wanted a way for him and his family to come and go without being bombarded by gamblers and attention seekers."

"Sounds like an amazing man." How often did she deal with those suffering from parental neglect or absent father and mother figures? More times than she could count on fingers and toes.

"He had me beat. Always spent time with me and cared about my future." His words were stunted and soft.

"I'm sorry for your loss."

Sig shook his head and adjusted his grip on the steering wheel. "I'm better now and it's been a year. Do you deal with a lot of death in your profession?"

Deflection, a well-known, well-practiced art by those who wanted to avoid their own emotions. She'd let him get away with it, for now. "Depends on how you define death. People, I say, are always facing some sort of death— whether personal or professional. It can be physical or emotional. It's non-discriminatory, really. When it comes to the dealing part, there is no right or wrong way, though I tell everyone peace terms must be set."

Silence ruled for the rest of the trip. They pulled into the casino parking lot twenty minutes after leaving the hotel. Lauren undid her seat belt, moved to open the door, but Sig snapped his fingers, grabbing her attention. "I'll get it."

He displayed his dominance again, opening not only the car door, but also the secret entrance, after pressing in the required key code. An elevator waited on the other side and they rode in the black, leather-lined interior up two floors.

She accepted his proffered treatment and let him wrap her arm in his, escorting her down a sterile, ivory-colored hallway with a red patterned carpet. Another door, another code and they entered a dark room. Her eyes adjusted and flitted over the wood desk and bookshelf, cherry leather loveseat and chair. Those things failed to command the attention of the room, they weren't the centerpiece. The objects served their purpose, but her focus turned toward the window overlooking the casino. People played slot machines and threw dice down a craps table. The glass spanned at least twenty-four feet and cast a glow over the whole room. Not enough to light it up like the casino floor, more like a nightlight projecting muted illumination. Sig didn't say anything, and she heard the door shut, the lock twist and click.

She stood mesmerized by wild, bright rush of life on the other side of the wall. No sounds or smells accompanied the view. There were people with smiles, frowns, and cups full of coins. A woman in the slinky, shimmering gold mini stopped to tug her breasts in place, while her male companion groped her ass. Emotions ran high on the other side of the wall and she loved being an observer rather than a participant.

Sig stood behind her and slid fingers up her arm, starting the warm spread of desire through two layers of fabric. "Let me take your coat."

Déjà vu all over again. Time to mix it up. She pointed at the monstrous window. "Is this what you wanted to show me?"

"Yes and no. I call it 'Art in Motion'. If you look out this window you can make up stories, like you'd do with any painting. Who are they, what fucked up problems they have, will they strike it rich, and so on. Sometimes I sit on the couch and watch."

"You people watch?" The concept, while not foreign or wholly inappropriate, appealed to her. A chance to be separate from interaction, yet still feel a part of life. While she cared about her clients, her job resembled people watching. She didn't give any of herself except her ears. In this case, her date gave his eyes. "And they see a mirror?"

"Correct. A reflection of themselves, and they either like it or hate it."

Easy to spend hours watching other people and weaving tales as opposed to evaluating their own problems. Glass clinked and ice fell. "Water?"

"Yes, please." Again his instincts were dead on. No guessing games, just accommodating her needs like at the hotel. "Tell me something, how do you know what I want?"

He extended the glass and she took it, held it. "Call it intuition. I'm tuned in to you."

"How long have you been living here?" She'd do the avoiding now. Talking about how they affected each other, or how he affected her, would be a Pandora's box better left shut. Instead, she'd ram against some more walls.

Chapter Five

"About eight months." Sig ran a free hand through his hair. "How did you know?"

Lauren turned away from the window. "The extra door, the kitchenette over in the corner. Besides, you people watch. I thought this might be your version of television."

He chuckled. She unlocked him faster than anyone else. These types of conversations were best left unsaid, and he had a laundry list of excuses for anyone who asked. Easier to get to work right away, saved money, since he'd refused to draw a salary until the books were back in positive numbers, and a convenient way for him to keep an eye on everything. Those false justifications wouldn't work with this one.

"You've got me all figured."

"Not yet." She paused and gulped down the last of the water. "I haven't determined one thing. Why the rope? You have control over every aspect of your life and you need control in the bedroom, too?"

The deep-seated anger rose up, not fast and furious as it did with other subs who 'didn't get bondage', or who considered his kink 'passive'. The ones who discriminated against kinks they didn't understand. How people labeled 'fucked up' by the general public still judged him because his kink fell into an uncommon category pissed him off.

Through his frustration he recognized, beyond any doubt, the ropes and the wrapping called to Lauren. Maybe not to the extreme level he liked and if anything she called him out because of her own fear.

"Let's get one thing straight. I bind people because it arouses me. I don't need to do it. I do it because I like it. Getting a hard dick isn't limited to ropes. Nails to my skin, a good grip on my balls, or simple biting can wind me up. But ropes—they are a true test of endurance, power, and patience. Not to mention, you bind a person up the right way and they look sexy as hell."

Her gaze wandered to her empty glass, the floor, everywhere but him.

"Do my words make you nervous?"

She made eye contact then. "A little."

"Why? And don't hold back. Don't lie to yourself to make this less messy. Half the people on the other side of the window fail at balancing the mess within themselves with the parts they consider normal. The ones who reconcile the bad with the good walk out of here with a profit of either monetary or mental satisfaction." He stepped forward, wrapping both palms around her one. She clenched the tumbler so tight her knuckles turned white. His warmth enveloped her and she relaxed her hold, relinquishing the glass with a little coaxing. He set it down on a small side table and stepped closer, cupping her face. "Lauren, you're beautiful and I know you can be one of the winners, grab hold of all the things you believe are chaotic and embrace them. They don't need to fit a mold."

"I'm nervous because I liked it and I'm not the type."

"How do you know? Maybe you're afraid to be anything but too vanilla."

She shook her head. "No, that's not it."

He let go of her, freeing her up to move and she did, pacing the length of the window, wringing her hands or swinging them back and forth.

She spoke while she moved. "What we did at the hotel... the way you talk to me, treat me, I've never experienced such a thing with anyone before. I've never been so emotionally naked."

A true confession and she started to scratch the surface of what a scene offered. "What we did isn't the deepest you can take it."

"There's more?"

"Let me show you."

***

Chaos and messy. The words played over in her mind along with Sig's offer. She already had a moment of extreme guilt a few minutes prior when she attempted to trivialize his desire to use ropes. And how incredibly wrong to try to minimize her reaction to his kink.

Yet she wanted to hold herself back, to keep some part of her from falling over the cliff. Victoria mentioned it to her, the ever-wonderful subspace. The place where the mind let go and gave over to sensation, to emotions. She'd been the one to keep things locked in place, to stay steady and firm. The woman in the mirror from the hotel wasn't one she recognized and— "All right, show me."

No sense in backing down. Her ex claimed she ran from opportunity. Even though every opportunity only dealt with giving him orgasms versus satisfying her own needs. This time the only out would be a safe word.

"Get the chair from the table and position it in front of the window."

The chair he'd pointed at had four wooden legs and armrests with a dark cloth seat. She dragged it over and then sat down, facing the one-sided mirror. People tossed the dice, the roulette wheel spun, and slot machines lit up with bright fluorescent bulbs.

"Take off everything." His words enflamed her, lit up her body like one of those slot machines and the room's temperature increased.

She followed the command, unzipping the boots first. While she removed her clothing, doors opened and shut behind her, and a loud thump reverberated through the room. Something told her not to turn, not to tempt her overactive imagination, and instead trust Sig to fulfill her cravings.

Once she finished her task, he spoke. "Turn and face me."

Nipples already hard, pussy damp, she responded by looking at him straight on. No shame in being naked, and his perusal told her he liked her this way.

"Perfect. Now stand there."

She wanted to talk, to ask if he'd explain everything to her like earlier, but she sensed a shift in him. He held a different kind of focus and concentration, efficiently undoing the rope chain he held and looping both ends. Fingers methodical, he fashioned three loops with a few tucks and pulls. Then he repeated the step with another length of nylon.

If she had a knife she'd be able to serve herself a slice of the sexual tension in the room. She focused on his actions and her breathing, slowly inhaling and exhaling to generate calm when her entire being stood on high alert in anticipation. Images of him caressing her the way he did the rope consumed her brain. Similar to their earlier scene, he took his time and then approached her.

"Lift one leg."

She brought one off the floor and he slid the nylon shackle upward, allowing the threads to abrade her calf and inspiring goosebumps to take up residence on her entire body. He stopped right above the knee, the heat from his palm soothing the minor scrapes he'd caused, and tightened the wrap. Then he did the same thing to the other leg.

Sensation became king when he gave the next instruction. "Get on your knees in the chair."

After she climbed up and closed her eyes, he tied the remaining lengths to secure her shackled limbs to each arm post at the front of the chair.

"Now place your arms flat against the armrests."

An easy command to follow, she watched him wrap and bind each forearm, melding it to wood and cloth. Her desire continued to grow, twisting inside her like a nut on a bolt. He executed meticulous focus and care to her body, trailing each finished piece with the tips of his fingers. Those little sensations did more than kisses, though she wanted those intimacies too. So far his ministrations included every part of her body except her face. He finished and stood before her. The question would be worth the punishment. "Would you kiss me now?"

He raised one eyebrow and leaned down, clasping her chin between two fingers. "Do you crave it?"

The question came out in a whisper, inches from her face. Mint, cedar and citrus blended together, a potent aphrodisiac assailing her nostrils. "Yes."

The first contact of his lips proved light, a mere press of skin to skin with no effort, so she darted her tongue out and licked the seam of his mouth. He retreated, frowning, his features at war with the desire in his eyes.

Then he launched an attack, a true plundering, nipping her sensitive skin and forcing his way through to explore. If his assault on her mouth said anything about his capabilities, then she'd die if he applied his skills to other parts of her body.

The kisses were shots of whiskey, flooding her with heat, want, and a million other emotions. Some she imagined weren't listed on her therapist feelings chart... carnal being one of them. When he broke away from her, stepping back and sitting on the coffee table behind him, they were both panting.

"For talking I'll have to punish you." He moved to his pants, releasing the buckle on his belt, and the button. Spreading the flaps wide, he slid his cock out of his briefs.

Her mouth dropped open and she swallowed a cry. A decent eight-inch length jutted out proudly, and he stroked from the head to the bottom of his shaft. A small drop of precum formed at the tip and her tongue swiped air, an offering. She wanted his cock in her mouth. Never excited about giving head before and it always seemed like a chore, but the idea appealed to her in this moment. A way to have control while at his mercy.

"Tell me what you want?" His question more a like a taunt as he continued to fondle himself.

"To taste you."

"Ah, but your punishment is to watch, not taste or feel. Imagine what you could be doing to me right now."

Oh, she did and she moaned when his head fell backward, nose pointed at the ceiling. His pace quickened, like he neared the end of a race, and when he gazed back at her the groan she produced matched his own. He let go of his cock and stalked toward her, circling behind her, thumping his length against her ass cheeks. The tear of foil ripped through the air, and he drew the covered head across the outer lips of her vagina, coating himself in her arousal. "Would you like to taste me now?"

She'd half a mind to say yes, and at the same time she wanted him to pound into her. To explore the limits of the chair and its ability to handle pressure—if she could handle it. She shook her head against the idea. He chuckled.

"No, you want me here." He thrust the head of his cock into her, and held there. At the same time he flicked her clit. A foreign sensation sent a sharp tingling along her neural pathways, which encouraged her to beg, to plead for release. She bit her lip in effort to keep silent.

Another inch, another flick and he continued the process until he fully seated his cock inside her. By then she'd become a whimpering, needy thing. She surprised herself by not pleading with him to put her out of her misery.

"How do you feel now?" His words were strained. They were both affected by his deliberate actions, and she'd discovered the end of her patience.

"Full and empty at the same time. I need movement, action."

He grabbed her hair, yanking her head back and nipping at her exposed throat. "If that's what you want."

"Yes," she growled.

He moved in fast, rough, and pounding strokes, in one second and out the next. She cried out at the sensations he evoked, unable to contain her desire to express herself. The ropes strained and stung, the pain intermixed with pleasure, acute and surprising. Her back went rigid when the orgasm burst forth, and Sig paused while her body shook from the release.

"My turn." He pulled out and moved in front of her. Condom gone and with cock in hand, he guided it to her mouth and she opened, flicking the tip with her tongue. She let him enter her, all hard, velvet heat. He wrapped both hands around her head, and steered her to the rhythm he enjoyed.

She relaxed her jaw and enabled his cock to make contact with the back of her throat. In a matter of mere minutes he went from absolute control to shouting expletives and dirty compliments at her. He shouted her name when he came, and she swallowed every last drop of his salty, earthy release. She licked her lips once he removed himself. Then he kissed her, leaning down and taking her mouth in a passionate, rough embrace. She warred with him, enjoying how he explored her with new passion, like he wanted to map the same passage his cock had occupied. His lips left hers and he pressed a gentle kiss to her forehead. "Thank you. This entire thing... beyond my expectations."

There were no more words and he moved away. When he came back he held a knife and a black silk robe. He cut the ropes. "There's a bathroom in my room off to the back, if you'd like a moment to yourself. Let me order a few things from the kitchen. I'm sure you're famished."

Signs of a true gentleman, he still took care of her, gave moments of privacy and offered refreshments. Sig held open the robe for her and she slipped her arms into the sleeves. "Thank you. Food sounds wonderful."

"Good. Take your time."

She gathered her clothes and started to reach for her boots when he whispered, "Leave everything where it is. You won't need any of those things for a few more hours."

Straightening, she took in his smirk and his visible state of arousal. "What can I expect?" Damn. She needed to learn about playing coy or at least not giving in so easily. But she craved anything he'd offer.

"I know some very practical ways to put the coffee table to good use. In fact, I'd like to have a feast from my table." He parted the folds of her robe and dragged two fingers across the juncture of her thighs.

"Fuck."

"With my tongue, yes. Of course, I did promise you a short break."

Lauren was at his mercy and in a world of trouble as the heat in her skin rose, no doubt putting a not-so-becoming blush on her cheeks. "Yes, I need a short break."

"Don't take too long or I may come after you." He went to his desk then, picking up the phone and barking out a command for room service.

Chapter Six

Ravenous. He repeated the word to the person taking his order on the phone. The best word to describe Lauren's effect on him. He'd lost all coherent thought when his cock had been buried inside her and damn near lost his entire mind when she'd swallowed every last bit of cum.

"Two orders of chocolate covered strawberries and a selection of fresh-cut tropical fruits. Anything else, sir?"

"Yes, add a bottle of champagne, too." Sig hung up the phone before the room service associate gave an acknowledging reply. No sense in wasting time on a conversation when he needed to start formulating his plans for the rest of the night, and check his rope stores. He thanked the heavens he'd moved his whole supply here, instead of leaving it languishing in storage.

She already had him doing things he never did in a scene. Sex didn't typically occur and even less common... the kissing. Her lips were heaven, her mouth addictive. Already just imagining her presence had him gripping the armrests of his chair, ready to launch and locate the very person who inspired the romantic musings he'd long believed lost to him. The evening had turned into more than just a scene. The challenge would be having it last longer than one night.

Dread filled him. Introducing her to his world, his uncle, and forcing her to live with his proclivities all at the same time— it'd never happen.

A heavy knock pounded on the office door, followed by Kanoa's deep voice. "I hope you're decent because I'm coming in."

The threat wasn't empty and he stalked into the room with an apologetic visage. Sig expected a tantrum, and got a sad giant instead.

"Why are you here?"

"There's been a situation. Your uncle made a few poor choices and—" Kanoa's eyes dragged toward the bedroom.

Lauren stood in the door, still wrapped in Sig's robe, her eyes wide and lips pursed in surprise. "Am I interrupting?"

"No." Sig motioned for her to come to him and she did, but they didn't have the remainder of the night now. "Where is my uncle?"

"In the penthouse suite. Your uncle baited another man into betting an evening of his wife's time for unlimited use of this penthouse suite is part of a friendly game. There's a temporary truce at the moment, but I don't know for how long. I've been looking for you for two hours."

"I'll head up there immediately. Go take point and let everyone know I'm on my way."

Kanoa nodded in acknowledgement and then left as fast as he arrived.

Sig took Lauren's hands in his. "I'm sorry. Looks like the coffee table will have to wait. In fact, maybe it's best to call it a night."

He didn't miss the hurt in her eyes, but too late to turn back. Too risky, as well. "I can have a car take you—"

"I thought you didn't like playing games. I understand you've got business to take care of, but it appears you're using it as an excuse to dismiss me." She wrenched away from him, gathering her clothes quickly.

"It's no game." The evening had been anything but, turning into the type of emotional flaying session he wanted to avoid. She'd wormed her way past all his defenses, found cracks in his armor. Made him want things he abandoned a year ago. It had to stop. Now. "My business requires my attention. I can't throw away the responsibility, not when I've worked so hard to restore this casino."

"Of course. When you've buried your feelings again then you can trust yourself, right? You wanted me to give myself up to the chaos, to the messy parts of me. Your words made the whole night...more. For lack of a better word, there's more here." She dropped the robe then, right in front of him, and stepped into her lace boy cut shorts, continuing to speak as each article of clothing found its way back onto her body. It became hard to focus when he wanted to take her right there, in all her righteous fury and fire. "Emotions are messy, and real interactions with people can be the same. Like kink, they can hurt. The pain equal to the pleasure means you're alive. Lock out those parts of ordinary, everyday things, push them away, and you'll be nothing more than a shell. As a therapist it's one thing I've learned the hard way. You can't expect to walk away from what we did without any effect—" She paused, tugging on her dress. Then she straightened her frame and faced him again. "I wish you'd at least given me the option to stay."

He took a deep breath, summoning his courage. Alpha in the bedroom and boardroom, but in this instance he found himself adrift like a roulette wheel without a dealer. "I can't."

She sighed and sat down, sliding her stocking feet into the

boots, her concentration on zipping them up. Frustrated, no doubt, and he readied for the yelling to start, except she did the exact opposite. No fit, no tantrum like other women he'd dated in years past. No tears, either. When she stood, her face represented calm personified, a mask of acceptance in place. "I'll leave you to take care of your business. Thanks for a nice evening. I can find my own way out and my own way home."

Her words wounded and cinched his gut like a tightening slip knot. Guilt gnawed. Yes, he lied again, but he didn't want to face the prospect of someone faking their interest in his kink and desires. Pretending to love him when they didn't. Still— "Lauren." He stepped out from the behind the desk, reached for her. "I'm not ready for more. This is all I have to give."

She gave a half-hearted smile. "Funny how when it's sex or a scene you expect trust, but you're not willing to trust others with anything. I'm no good at being in one-sided arrangements, Sigmund."

"I'm not asking you to be." Damn. He'd survived so far, and she was the unlucky one who got him for his first scene in a year. It must be why he'd gone off the deep end, suckered into something so much more. Cutting ties would be for the best.

She put on her coat, hugging the flaps together and flipping up the collar. "Then you understand when I tell you I won't settle for less than equal emotional engagement."

"I understand."

She walked out the door.

He stood there for a few minutes trying to figure out how he could get her back. Shaking his head, he turned his focus to the mess with his uncle. They needed to finish this once and for all. The pain dulled, anger covering up most of the mess. No time to wallow.

***

Lauren kept her composure until she climbed into the back of the cab. She got the name of the hotel out before her eyes blurred and tears tracked down her face. The cold, distant asshole she left acted the complete opposite of the searching, caring man she'd arrived with. No, he ran scared at the mention of giving any more of himself to her, though he'd asked for all of her.

She'd given blindly, letting him truss her up and do things, calling to the parts of her she longed to hide. When he'd called out her name, she lost a bit of herself to him. He represented so many things she wanted— a safe harbor for her desires and a chance to find refuge from the strains of her job. Sure, it was ridiculous to expect a full relationship to emerge from one night, but at least she was willing to entertain the prospect. He'd awoken emotional needs in her and then ripped away the security blanket he offered before she had a chance to come to terms with everything. The idea of facing the aftermath alone had her hugging herself in the backseat of the cab, sobbing and shivering.

"Ma'am, are you all right?"

"Fine," she said between sniffles. "Just cold."

"I'll turn up the heat, then."

The warmest furnace wouldn't mend her aching chest, or the painful throb that took up residence the moment Sig turned away from her. It would only serve as a reminder of how she got burned.

She'd enjoy the rest of the night in the hotel suite, maybe take a nice long bath to soak away her misgivings. He'd awakened her desires. Time to consider how to handle them and her future without him.

***

Sig stalked to the elevator, pounded the keys, and damn near assaulted the steel walls. When the doors opened to the penthouse suite, he'd calmed himself marginally. Two security officers stood outside the entrance, and one clasped a doorknob, holding the door open for him. Still too pissed to talk, his thank you came out more like a grunt.

The room, white and bright, gave the impression of heaven. Cream-colored walls, carpets and furniture, all trimmed in gold. Yet God didn't sit on the couch. His uncle sat there in a brocade robe, dress trousers, and slippers, smoking a cigar with one hand and grasping a glass of whiskey in the other.

"I'll be damned if my nephew hasn't decided to grace me with his presence."

He chose not to respond just yet. Instead he sat down on the opposite love seat, sinking into the cool, microsuede surface. "Evening, Ed. Mind telling me why my bodyguard interrupted my date?"

His uncle shrugged. "No clue. I had a friendly game of Texas Hold'em with your CEO friend."

"Really? I think our definitions of friendly are in opposition."

Sig would admit he ignored his uncle's antics for too long. In his grief he didn't want to deal with anyone else's. He'd done his duty by bringing Isle of Bermuda back from the brink.

"It's a game. People can wager whatever they want."

"Yes, but this suite isn't yours to wager. I've let you stay here out of respect for my father. You've used the time to alienate multiple whales and put my restoration project at risk. Why?"

"You're killing this place," Ed growled. "You're a young pup, with no respect for the older generation. Before Bernard's death you were always gallivanting around, going to those kink clubs. Now you lock yourself off, pander to the young crowd, even opening a nightclub in the casino." Pushing off the couch, his uncle paced back and forth. "All I want is to offer some alternatives, have a voice like I did with your father, but you don't listen."

"And you trying to ruin relationships with the whales I am attracting shows me I should listen?" Sig stood too, fists clenched. The man had balls trying to call him out, when he'd done nothing but live off the casino for the entire year.

His uncle stopped and faced him, eyes filled with hurt. "You wouldn't give me the time of day, otherwise. I tried coming to the office, but your muscle always told me you weren't available. Your father's not the only one who devoted a lot to this casino. But trying to get a meeting with you over food— impossible. Running into you on the floor, the opportunities were few and far between. Those moments I did get, you always cut me off before giving me a chance."

A rock lodged itself into Sig's stomach as the instances replayed in his mind. Sure he'd brushed his uncle off, but not because he didn't care. More like he cared too much and the best way to avoid personal conversations was to bury himself in work.

"You've grown cold, son." Ed walked around the table and put a hand on his shoulder. "Untouchable and detached. You're so lost in everything I started to worry I'd lose you, too."

"Really?"

Ed pulled him into a stiff hug.

His initial reaction was to push away, but then his uncle whispered in his ear. "This whole thing...I just wanted to get your attention. To have a chance."

The hug meant something then, and guilt swamped him. He loosened his limbs and gripped his uncle tight. "You've got it."

Several throats cleared and the two men separated. Expressing emotions needed to be kept brief, after all, appearances were required.

"All right, so my whale is fine?"

"No, but I'll smooth those edges myself if you'll give me a chance."

"Here's your shot, Uncle. Don't screw it up."

"I won't and I'm sorry for taking you away from whatever you were working on."

He'd been working all right, and the reminder of Lauren's face, angry and frustrated, popped into his mind. Damn. If he hadn't given her the same treatment he delivered to those closest to him, maybe she'd still be in his office right now. The one person not willing to put up with the shit he dished out was Kanoa, probably due to their past, best buds and repaying debts—crap not easily tossed aside. Others hadn't gone those extra miles and to be honest they shouldn't have had to.

"Uncle?"

"Yes?"

He clasped Ed on the shoulder, "Can we continue our conversation tomorrow, over dinner?"

His uncle laughed. "Really? No backing out this time."

"I won't, I'll make sure reservations are at The Triangle. I'd like your thoughts on the place, since I'm thinking about a remodel."

"Sounds great."

"You'll fix things with the whale?" He walked backwards toward the door.

"I'll take care of it. Get out of here and enjoy the rest of your night."

He crossed his fingers and made for the elevator. Maybe she went back to the hotel. If so, he'd have a chance to apologize. She deserved an apology. No, she deserved a hell of a lot more.

"You need anything?" Kanoa asked.

"No, unless you've got some good advice on how to win a woman back."

His bodyguard chuckled. "I'm the wrong person to ask, but good luck."

***

Lauren sat down on the couch and picked up the glass of red wine, remnants of the bottle they'd opened during dinner. It helped, along with the other relaxation tactics she'd employed since arriving back at the hotel room. A hot bath, a glass of wine, and now... hell, she didn't know what to do. Her mind wandered back to Sig and his strange behavior, which reminded her to be thankful he'd shown his true colors. He gave her the best orgasm of her life and mind-blowing sex, but still— A knock at the door echoed with a staccato beat, followed by an additional three solid taps in rhythm.

Better answer it, in case it was someone with the hotel. She glanced through the peephole—holy shit! Sig stood on the other side, an extra button on his collar undone, hair ruffled, with a frown. He raised his arm to knock again and she hesitated, but curiosity got the best of her. One question—she had to know.

"What do you want?"

He lowered his arm. "A chance to apologize. To explain my attitude earlier."

"Go on."

He tugged on a tuft of his hair. No wonder it appeared messy. The image of the crisp, composed, businessman long gone. "Is there any chance I could explain things without including the entire hotel floor?"

A bit exaggerated, she doubted every room had occupants and if there were people in every room, they had more interesting things to do. Regardless, she found herself flipping the top lock and opening the door. She moved with it, stepping back to allow him inside, and shut the only barrier keeping them apart. When she turned to acknowledge him, he'd already taken up position on the chair, elbows on his knees.

Walking over, she sat across from him on the coffee table. The urge to reach out and hold him overwhelmed her. For some reason she wanted to offer comfort, with an instinct to be a rock for the wayward or tortured soul.

"What did you need to say?"

His eyes searched hers. "I'm not good at embracing people. Tonight I found out I'm not good at relationships at all and my uncle, of all people, had to practically get me to kick him out of the casino to get my attention. You wanted my acknowledgement that you are worth my time, and you deserve to be treated like your time is valued. I threw it away for a shitty reason."

"I'm still not sure what you mean."

Sig chuckled. "No, I'm not making much sense." He shoved himself up to a standing position, grabbing her hands. "Your time is worth something, and I'm sorry for not showing you earlier, in my office, how much I appreciated you giving it to me." He leaned down and pressed a kiss to one set of knuckles. "Along with your body." Another butterfly caress of lips on skin to the other set. "And your trust."

Letting go of her, he sat back down. "Thank you."

She remembered to breath, the tenderness and the love—yes, she knew how love appeared and somehow he possessed it for her—visible in each kiss and in his unwavering gaze. "Thank you."

He cocked his head to one side. "For what?"

"For showing me the part of you into bondage and the parts you've been hiding from everyone else."

She stood, interlocking their fingers and tugging. "Follow me."

They walked over to the bedroom door, and she stopped there, let go and gazed at him.

"What do you want?" His question came with narrowed eyes. He'd taken over control again, which suited her fine.

"You, naked. Show me all of you." A true test in her opinion, since every sexual and bondage scene they'd had this evening resulted in him keeping the majority of his clothes intact, like battle armor.

He shed the coat, the shoes, the socks, and then— "Undo the buttons on my shirt."

The command spawned immediate arousal and she reached forward, following his order. She tempered her inner desire to rush, to hurry this along and expose his chest. Instead, she took her time, using it to determine if this was what she wanted.

Did she believe his words? They'd both been played or hurt by ones they loved. In some ways, they'd both lost big when it came to relationships. Her gut told her he wouldn't risk this much for a simple screw.

"You can trust me. I need you, not sex... not ropes. I plan to take you. No games, no mindfuck. Just me, in your body."

She shook her head. "That's not what I crave." Pausing from her current task, she took one of his tanned, long-fingered hands and wrapped it around her wrist. "I like how I look bound by you. You wrapped around me is sexier than without any bondage at all."

He released her, and those fingers cupped her chin. "So you want my ropes."

"As much as I want you."

***

Inside the dam broke, and Sig yanked her against his body and into a kiss, sharp, hot, with dueling tongues. She gave him another chance and then confessed to being into his kink, to desiring it like he did. This woman represented a blessing. He had to show her. He pulled back and she whimpered with blatant desire. Her nipples pebbled against the thin purple fabric of her robe. No doubt she was already wet for him.

"Take off the robe and sit on the coffee table."

She walked away, trailing her fingernails along his abdomen

and his eager cock jerked in his pants.

He went into the bedroom to retrieve his ropes and strip from his clothes. When he returned to the living room, she'd perched herself on the one end of the rectangular wood table, facing away from him with her hair loose and reaching the middle of her back. Legs crossed, she swung a foot in the air making small circles. He dropped the two skeins of rope on the table.

The thud had her glancing at him over her shoulder with a knowing smile, then her jaw dropped. "You're gorgeous."

Heat bloomed in his cheeks. A woman made him blush. "Silence, remember, or you get punished."

"If punishment involves your body, I'll take it."

"You read my mind." He stared down at her. She reached up with those long fingers, dragging her nails across his straining erection. "Lay back."

Lust blazed her eyes, but she did as he asked, flat on her back, exposed and magnificent, her pert breasts with rock-hard nipples saluting the air. He started to kneel but bent instead to pay homage and suckle her. His hands were already working both chains loose. He planned to work fast, for some reason his patience had been stretched thin. But he didn't want to disappoint, not after she expressed her love for the bondage.

Pressing kisses to her stomach he followed his own trail across her soft skin, until he reached her golden curls, nuzzling them to smell her. He licked her arousal from the tip of his nose, and then proceeded to swipe at her sex, from the slit to the clit. She shivered, but remained silent.

Trained well at multi-tasking, he grasped her ankle and backed it against a table leg, then wound the rope around both, in at least four loops. Probing her vulva with his tongue, he wound the nylon and tied off one end, securing the first ankle.

From there everything went wild. She moaned and he lost the urge to finish binding her until she came. He switched to sole clit stimulation, shoving two fingers roughly inside her. She bucked against his mouth, and then her back arched, crying out his name when she came, her vaginal walls milking his fingers. The sounds, the sensations, became too much. He wanted to take her now.

He untied and discarded the ankle binding, then pulled her up off the table.

Face flushed and gaze confused, she shook her head slowly. "Why are you stopping?"

"I need you. Need to see you ride me."

***

Sig fell back on the couch with Lauren on top, straddling him. She reached for him drawing his cock between both palms. He was fire, velvet, and steel all-wrapped-in-one. He'd pleasured her, drove her fucking insane. Yes, she wanted to swear in six different ways at how he set her afire, making her buck like some desperate, wild thing, and then denying her the full tie-up adventure. Yet, she understood his need to be close. The same yearning clawed at her mind, too.

She slid off him, down to the floor, never letting go of his cock. She traced the tip with her tongue. A drop of precum emerged like an early present and she lapped it up. His fist wrapped in her hair, but he let her lead. She didn't swallow him whole, recalling his earlier statement labeling himself a Dom and a masochist. He liked to be denied, and deny she did. Tracing the length of him with her tongue, down one side and up the other before he tugged on her hair and she stopped.

He held out a wrapped condom. "Get up here."

She obeyed, letting her pussy hover and tease. For a faint moment she imagined them together exclusively and him driving into her bareback. She imagined his tan hands tracing her pale belly, large with child. Sure, a little bit rushed, but they were visions she'd avoided with her ex. Sig inspired crazy ideas and wild notions she'd never entertain under normal circumstances.

"Put the condom on me."

A slow, torturous stretch, and he hissed when she massaged him, rolling the latex down the length of his shaft. Fire burned in those dark brown eyes and he gripped her waist, squeezing tight before he guided her down. She tried to fight against him as he entered her, a torture all its own, wanting his cock to pound inside her passage. But those firm arms kept her from achieving the desperate fullness she craved.

Half-inch by half-inch he submerged into her, gaze locked on hers. She'd been trying to stay silent, except her mouth kept opening subconsciously, wanting to speak out. To beg.

"Tell me." Sig, the fucking masochist, wanted her to vocalize.

So she did. "I want you to fuck me, please. So hard I'll remember this for weeks."

He drew a sharp breath and for a moment everything stopped. Then he kissed her, rough and messy. Tongues, teeth, and lips desperate for connection... for taste. When they broke apart he slammed his cock all the way into her.

As he drove in and out, she marveled at how he fit her as if made for her pussy alone. Coupled with the rhythm were his fingers digging into her hips, no doubt leaving marks. He added to the pain by biting her shoulder, hard. Her body tensed and her brain went fuzzy, like how she felt right before going to sleep. A plane where nothing existed except pleasure, and all stood at peace.

How long it continued she didn't know. This time when her orgasm crested and a keening cry left her lips, she saw stars, everything more vivid than her last release. He came at the same time, jerking against her body and holding her tight against him.

Lauren collapsed against his shoulder, spent.

All too soon he moved her, positioning her on the couch before he left. She closed her eyes to rest, a smile on her face. Sig symbolized perfection. Demanding, thoughtful, and everything she wanted. Even his mistakes endeared her, since he'd learned from them, unlike others.

A warm cloth caressed her leg and her lover's voice spread over her like syrup on pancakes. "Let me clean you up."

She spread her legs, allowing him access and he administered to her as one would to someone they love. "Do you do this for all your subs?"

"No, because most of them I never slept with."

Her eyes flew open when he slid both arms under her. "What are you doing?"

"Taking you to bed," he replied with a smile.

Once inside the bedroom, he laid her down and pulled the covers up. The sheets were cool against her skin and sprouted gooseflesh everywhere they touched. Turning off the lights, he climbed in beside her. A domestic moment, for sure. One she easily imagined happening every night.

"Are you serious about this...us?" She waited, unable to face him. Maybe he changed his mind.

He grabbed her shoulders and tugged. Rolling with the motion, she faced him. "Lauren." Her name sounded like a plea. "I can't think of anything I crave more."

They curled up then, entwining legs and arms. He pressed soft kisses to her forehead and cheeks, before giving one final command. "Sleep, so we can have more adventures tomorrow."

What You Want

Dedication

To Mai Cate, who always inspires me to reach out for the craziest ideas and make them work. Also, to my inspirational husband for another idea worth putting to paper.

What You Want

When her sister gets sick on the night of her 1Night Stand date, Laney Malcolm is asked to fill in and pretend to be her twin. Treating it as a lark, she looks forward to an adventurous event with a free dinner and not much else. She isn't prepared for the fierce attraction nor the urge to help the Hawaiian, tattooed submissive she's introduced to.

Kanoa Mahelona has spent the last year trying to find himself, but he's tired of random hook-ups and women who only want him for his bad-boy image. Madame Eve helped his boss, so he turns to her for assistance. Attractive and damn good at breaking through his barriers, the blonde Domme challenges him in a way he can't seem to turn down.

Only she's not who she appears to be, and, once the truth comes out, it may be too late to go back.

Chapter One

"I don't think I can go."

Laney Malcolm pulled her head out of her book, staring at her sister propped up in the doorway. "Go where?"

"My date tonight," she replied with a sniffle. "Can you go for me?" Lacey looked miserable, hair flat, eyes and nose red, and a blue terrycloth bathrobe wrapped around her sweats and tank top getup. Resembling nothing like the neat, well-put-together woman she'd lived with all her life. Literally, since the womb.

From the moment they both popped out of their mother, Laney had been the messy, carefree one, while her big sister—of two whole minutes—believed in tight control, order, and clean presentation, which was exactly why her sister never entered her clothes-everywhere domain. She lounged on her nice comfortable bed, unmade and perfect with its mismatched sheets. "Why should I bother? Just call and cancel."

"There's a no refund policy for cancellations under forty-eight hours. I'm supposed to be there in one hour. I've heard he's a sweet guy."

A single word, so often paired with innocence, piqued her interest. As a sexual Dominant, she enjoyed making nice, vanilla guys bad. As a voyeur and exhibitionist, she loved pushing buttons and challenging limits. "What do you know?"

"Not a lot, but Madame Eve doesn't work with felons or people of questionable behavior."

"Lace, are you trying to get me to believe you know nothing about this guy?" The concept seemed impossible because her twin had to know everything about people, down to their tax bracket, before she did more than take them for a romp in her dungeon.

"You always tell me I'm too controlling, and Victoria encouraged me to put faith in the system."

"Come again? Victoria put you up to this?" True, their fellow Dominant tended to push people into situations they were too afraid to pursue themselves. That's what made her so good at breaking people. But, Laney didn't want her sister taking unnecessary risks, even if she did use the word control a little too often when it came to describing her sister's penchant for managing every small detail.

Lacey rolled her eyes and locked her hands on her hips. "Another glaring reminder of how you don't listen. To anyone. At their wedding a few weeks ago, she finally told me the truth about how she found Royce again, and Madam Eve's 1Night Stand service was responsible. I told you this during the reception. Anyways, so I signed up and told them the only thing I wanted to know about my date is a name and three facts. This way I can't overthink or anything."

She nearly burst out laughing at her twin's proclamation but settled for a smile instead as said counterpart began coughing up a lung. "Obviously, Mother Nature put a wrench in the last bit of control you had over the whole experience."

"Don't be a witch. Please help me. Besides it's only a date. You don't have to sleep with him, and he's a new sub."

Even better. Twins were the devil. "Tell me more."

Lacey grinned. "His name is Kanoa. He's Hawaiian, born on the second-biggest island, has tattoos, and likes riding horses. P.S., he's still figuring out his kinks."

Interesting combination. He wanted to learn more about the life. Damn, she wasn't the best of teachers, and it'd be crazy to do something this stupid. Yet, she'd always been a sucker for caramel-skinned men and tattoos. "Give me one good reason to pretend I'm you."

"Because I'd do the same for you."

Laney shook her head. "It'll cost you more than a guilt trip."

"You're shrewd."

"They don't call me Pretty Woman for nothing." No, in fact they gave her the nickname because she refused to kiss her submissives, especially since the last boyfriend broke her heart. Kisses were for those you wanted relationships with, not a good time. "Your loss. I'm happy to stay curled up all comfy at home doing—"

"Fine. I'll broadcast my next two dungeon visits."

Now the sacrifice would be worth it. Her sister had a way with domination. In fact, she was a damn queen at it. To watch her act out a scene with any sub served as training session all on its own. No sexual play, just the scene—a sub in the height of sensual deprivation, big sis's expertise. Laney merely enjoyed calling the shots in the place she'd grown most comfortable—the bedroom. She'd give of herself all day, but the dungeon and a good scene were where she owned every word, every movement. "What does he know about you?"

"My entire application, including pictures."

"So, I'd be you."

"Yes and no." Lacey sniffled and pulled a tissue from her robe pocket to wipe her nose. "Job wise and interests would be mine, but you may want to be more dominant than you usually are...outside of the scenes."

She could do this. "All right, fine. But three broadcasts."

"Whatever." Her sister waved a hand in the air. "Now, what are you going to wear?"

"I thought this would work." She glanced down at her baby doll, hot-pink T-shirt and fuzzy, striped lounge pants. The outfit served as a mood killer for sure. The date could wrap fast and then she'd be back to finish her latest library borrow before ten o'clock.

"Be serious. Grab your faded jean skirt over there on the floor, near the bathroom door, and the jean vest from the chair. Have you shaved your legs recently?"

"Yes, Mom. And why do you want me to look good?"

Her twin threw the used tissue at her. "You're representing me, damn it."

Laney grudgingly set her book on the nightstand, got up, and grabbed the suggested clothing. "I hate all this subterfuge crap, and I'm wearing my boots." Not an option or up for debate. Getting roped into a blind date with some tattooed sub meant she'd need something on her body to play the part of comfort clothing. Her spurred boots fit the bill. "Why don't I just tell him the truth?"

"Good question. Go for it if you want."

"That's it?" She questioned her twin's sudden change of heart. The girl had been a manipulating, bargaining piece of work since childhood.

"I wouldn't want you to go against yourself. To be honest, he won't be able to tell us apart. I'm not going to hold you to anything, but it might be fun pretending to be someone else for the night."

Laney slipped into her leather boots, the antique spurs jingling as she did. *I can't believe I'm doing this.* A quick comb through her hair, a clip to pull back the long bangs from her face, a swipe of mascara, a coat of "pinky sparkle" lip gloss, and she was ready. "How do I look?"

"Like Cowgirl Barbie."

Good enough for her.

***

A sharp rap sounded on his hotel room door.

Kanoa peeked through the peephole and swore before

disengaging the chain lock and opening up. "What the hell are you two doing here?"

Stepping back, he let his best friend and boss, Sig, and Sig's fiancée, Lauren, into the room. His friend spoke first. "Thought we'd wish you good luck tonight."

Then she did. "And tips."

"I didn't know I needed any." He tugged at the bottom of his black button-down silk shirt.

"Well, if we're talking body guarding or military, I'd say no. You're an expert, and I know that from experience. But your recent track record is more hook up than put up."

He raised an eyebrow at his boss. "I—"

"Give me a chance to say two things." Lauren reached out to fold down the unruly edge of his collar.

He nodded.

"One, you're intimidating. Two, you don't say much."

Because he learned more by being silent. Case in point. "And how should I stop those two things."

His buddy since their first day of boot camp clapped him on the shoulder and smiled. "Put a grin on your face, like so."

Lauren took over. "And don't cross your arms during dinner. Keep them open. Encourage questions. Open yourself up to answering anything."

Kanoa pursed his lips.

"Don't look at her like she's a plain civie with no clue," Sig replied, pulling his girl in close. "She's the therapist."

"Yes, and my therapy sessions tell me most women and men want people in their lives without a ton of secrets."

The moment those two shared between them reminded him of why he'd signed up for this date in the first place—to find someone to talk to. To find a friend. Sure, he had the people in this room, but he didn't believe in crossing the line between friend and employer. It just wasn't in him, even if he'd been buddies with Sig in the military. When the man became his boss, the lines changed. As for women, his type of relationships could be boiled down to a simple exchange of physical pleasures. Anything more than a romp in the hay seemed fishy, especially with the type of women he met on the job. Tonight would involve some major soul searching. He only hoped the woman Madame Eve had set him up with turned out to be the real deal and not another faker seeking a hot body covered in tats.

"I'll give it my best shot."

"Wow," his boss said with wide eyes.

"What?"

They chuckled before Lauren spoke, "We didn't know how you'd take all this."

"I take it as you both care about me and I appreciate it." He gave a small smile, not a full-blown, world-ending deal, but something to at least show them no hard feelings.

"Holy shit, he smiled. First one I've seen in a couple of months." The boss man tugged his woman toward the door then. "We'll get out of your hair. Have a wonderful night, and I hope it ends with a good romp in this room."

I'd settle for a talk.

Chapter Two

Laney pulled into the parking lot of the Luau's Hawaiian Grill, and found herself not impressed. She'd expected the selected restaurant to have some sort of class, possibly style. Not a hole-in-the-wall, strip-mall joint looking like it pulled its booths together from a restaurant supply surplus auction.

A small line had formed inside, so obviously they served decent food. Damn if she hadn't committed the same sort of church-going, book-cover judging she'd called so many others out on before. Determined to correct her initial error, she took the key out of her Jeep, inhaled and exhaled a few calming breaths then headed inside.

First impressions brought no fuzzy feels as she glanced around at the fake palm trees and surfer motif. But the smells.... Some heavenly scent, spices and pineapple, came from the kitchen, and her stomach gave a little growl of appreciation.

"Lacey?" Her sister's name came out silky smooth like creamy peanut butter spread on toast, and she turned for a glimpse at her date. He stood a hell of a lot taller than her, not a tattoo in sight, and his black hair had been slicked back into a ponytail. Clean-shaven, with a black dress shirt, jeans, and black boots..

"Kanoa?"

"You pronounced it right." His chocolate-brown eyes softened.

She smiled wide in return. "I can't lie and say I didn't look it up. It's a bitch when people pronounce your name wrong, am I right? Personally, it makes me feel a bit underappreciated, and when you deal with people every day, all day, I think taking a few minutes to make them not just another face in the crowd is important."

Here she went rambling and cussing, but the endless, profane chatter seemed to do the trick because his shoulders relaxed and the arms crossed above his chest fell loose. "I tend to lose respect for people who don't say my name correctly. No sense in showing them any care when they don't return the courtesy."

A stab of guilt twisted in her side. Lying didn't show respect, either. "Kanoa, I—"

"Are you hungry?" He obviously hadn't heard her pitiful attempt at a confession. "This line gets long pretty fast, and I want to make sure we get a good seat."

Laney shook her head. "You're too much of a gentleman. Don't know what I'm going to do with you, but I'm famished."

He extended an arm, sleeve sliding up to give her a glimpse of tattoos hiding underneath. She scooted ahead of him to the back of the line. Huddled near the bamboo half-wall separating the ordering line from the eating area, she decided not to give the conversation a chance to dull or her own bad choices to keep replaying in her mind. "How long have you been living in the area?"

"I've been here for a few years."

Short, succinct, and to the point. "And before then?"

He stared ahead over her head, either to scan the menu or for the simple purpose of avoiding connection. "The military owned me from high school graduation until two years ago."

While this sentence was longer, she saw no sense in continuously putting herself out there. They always said the best dancing came when a partner showed up, and, so far, Kanoa didn't want to tango. So she moved forward with the line and twirled the ends of a lock of her hair between two fingers. When they were about three customers from the ordering window, she'd reached her limit. "You don't want to be here do you?"

Her question got his attention because those melt-into-me eyes went from focusing on the menu to linking with hers. "Excuse me?"

"You heard me correctly. We've been in line for approximately ten minutes with only me initiating conversation. Your responses are no more than a few sentences long. So, I'll ask you again, do you want to be here with me?" She never raised her voice. Ever. Something she'd learned from her Dominant mentor. Elevated tonality did nothing to encourage conversation or obedience, but clear, concise words felled people like a saw to a tree trunk.

He cleared his throat, and gave his collar a tug. "I can't say I'm good at conversation. It's never been my strong suit really."

Her sister's words replayed in her head about being more controlling than normal. Laney didn't typically summon those skills outside a dungeon. Yet, something about this big man's hesitance, and subtle fear, called to the Dominant in her. The need to put him at ease by taking out the guesswork. Therefore, she'd do exactly that.

"I can understand where you're coming from. Sometimes I'm not into conversing either. Let's throw the pressure cooker out the window, then, and go for something simple. How about every time I ask you a question you have to answer with more than a sentence? If you can't, then I get one bite of your dinner."

A black eyebrow went up.

"What? Is there something wrong with my suggestion?"

"No, but you don't look like you eat much. Unless you're a food binger or suffer from an eating disorder. Damn, now I've insulted you."

Laney touched his arm, the initial contact sparking a latent desire. Something she'd rather not be interested in right now. This guy needed her help and reassurance, not her lust. "Nope, not insulted. It takes a lot more than completely hypothetical statements to get me roiling. And kudos to you, already trying my game. I also eat a ton of food. The games I like to play require a girl to keep her stamina up."

Like no big thing, the line disappeared and it was their turn to order. Unfortunately, she'd spent all her time focusing on Kanoa instead of the menu. When the man behind the register asked her what she wanted, she replied, "I honestly don't know. What's the most popular item on the menu?"

"Tonight's special is kalua pork and I highly recommend it," her date leaned over and whispered. "It comes with two sides."

"Which ones?" She asked, reveling in having him close and advising her. Her own guardian, hulking shadow.

"A cabbage-ramen salad and potato-macaroni salad."

She'd never tried either, but tonight was all about new experiences. *Why the hell not?* "I'll have the kalua pork special."

Stepping aside, she took her glass from the counter and shuffled to the beverage dispensers. Filling her glass with water, she then grabbed utensils and extra napkins and selected a booth not too far from the door for them to sit in.

Kanoa walked over with the number card to identify their meal. "Should be out shortly. Thank you for grabbing everything. I'm horrible at this. I can't think of anything else to say." He sat down, the seat shrinking beneath him.

"It's all right." She pushed her hair behind her shoulder. "I can help in that area since you already know everything about me. The only thing I know about is your culture and fondness for riding horses. Tell me more."

"The culture or the horses?"

"Both."

He smiled, big and wide. "Sounds good to me. I can start with the horses. A friend owns a few, and I ride whenever I can. I like being on horseback, traveling across the terrain and feeling the power conveying you to your destination. There's no experience like it, except maybe riding a motorcycle."

"Do you have a motorcycle?"

The question appeared to light a fire within him, transforming his nervousness and melting away the shy exterior. "Yes, I own a Shadow Spirit. Painted black, and I've got a few talismans for protection etched into the handle bars. Where I'm from, superstition tends to be a way of life. No sense in taking chances, so I make sure to honor my ancestors and familial beliefs. I don't have a car."

"Good thing I do."

They both chuckled.

"Yes, I remember, a silver Taurus. I didn't see it in the parking lot. Then I recalled your info and you mentioned your sister drove the Jeep."

The guilt fork twisted in her stomach. This man seemed too perceptive for his own good. "Yes, she had a full gas tank. Tell me something in Hawaiian."

"*U'i mukana, ku'wipo.*"

Laney loved the way the words rolled off his tongue. "What does it mean?"

"Beautiful gift, sweetheart."

A blush bloomed on her cheeks, and she waved her hand in front of her face. "Is everyone so forward where you come from?"

"Not really and it's a compliment. I can't say I've had interesting dinner companions in a long time."

Instead of responding, she took a drink of water and tried to gain control of her body's response to Kanoa's flirting.

"Have you ever ridden a motorcycle before?"

Thankful for the change of subject, she shook her head. "Can't say I have. But horses...I've spent plenty of time on them. In fact, my daddy's brother owns a ranch right north of the Arkansas and Missouri state line. I try to spend time up there when I can."

"Well, maybe we can remedy your lack of experience on motorcycles after dinner?"

"Maybe I don't take rides whenever they are offered?" She'd let him read a little deeper into her innuendo. This conversation seemed to be opening him up a lot more than she'd expected, except he was showing her only a partial of himself.

He shrugged. "Can you blame me for wanting to do something with you that you've never done? There's something fantastic about feeling the wind in your hair, watching everything pass by without a sheet of glass separating you from it. I purchased my first hog years ago on my home island. Gas isn't cheap when you live away from the mainland. I rode it everywhere. Sold the bike when I joined the military and then, as soon as I got out, bought the one I have now."

The way he talked, the passion inflected in his words and the animation of his face, told her those memories were some of his favorites. These thoughts were true ones, without artifice. He liked to be free, which made his interest in submission odd. A fellow freedom seeker, she'd been drawn to the dominant side of things. She got a rush from calling the shots in all aspects of her life, though she typically deferred to friends and family about decision-making outside of the bedroom. She'd already done it tonight, by letting Kanoa select her dinner option. "Sounds exhilarating and maybe I'll let you introduce me to it."

As her words settled in, the food showed up. Each plate piped hot steam into the air and smelled absolutely wonderful. They dug in and let the silence linger as they ate. Until Kanoa lifted a forkful of his teriyaki chicken and extended it toward her mouth. "Here's a bite to make up for my one-sentence questions and answers."

"You remembered the rules." She opened for the tasty morsel, and the sweet tang of the sauce, mixed with chargrill flavor, melted on her tongue. "Delicious." He seemed surprised she let him feed her, judging by his wide eyes and hesitance in lowering the fork to her mouth. Such intimate acts floated outside of her sister's realm of accepted actions. Lacey didn't get down with being fed or doted upon.

Laney thrived on touch and believed in the healing power that came from placing hands on someone's skin. Hard to get rid of the natural reactions she experienced whenever in the company of someone else.

Pulling back, Kanoa speared another small piece of chicken and extended it. This time she reached for the fork. Without hesitation, she connected against him the rest of the way, sliding her fingers up his arm. The coarse hairs smoothed at her touch and the bumps of his wrist bones were more pronounced. Finally she trailed along his fingers and grasped the handle of the plastic fork. The entire process lit a fire in those brown eyes of his, and she grinned. "Thank you for following the rules and for complimenting me."

"I live to please. Though I expected you to be more likely to withhold things than embrace them."

"Better to give a taste of potential, the bare promise of more." She'd become rather adept at giving logical reasons for why she acted nothing like her sister. *Here's to hoping he doesn't catch on.*

After Laney returned the fork, they ate in silence for at least five minutes, but her bites were small, deliberate. The air around them thickened with sexual tension, so thick a dropped plate in the kitchen had her jumping in her seat. The noise brought her back to the present, to her goal. No more fooling around. "If you've read my profile, you know I'm a Dominant. Does the concept appeal to you?"

"Yes, very appealing. I've been interested in the lifestyle for a while, but I'm not sure what I want out of it. To be honest, I've never participated in a scene. I've watched a few and understand the rules. But physically allowed my submission? Never."

They locked eyes. He'd uttered a word she despised. "Don't use that word please."

"What word?"

"Never. Can't stand the word because every time I've used it, I do the exact thing I swore I'd never do."

He grinned. "All right, I can keep the N word under wraps. But I'm afraid, when I use it, I follow through."

Interesting, since he'd been submitting to her all night, and again he posed a challenge she naturally wanted to win. For some reason, this hulking male specimen called to her primal dominance. She'd like to see him stick his foot in his mouth. "Really? Well, what if I told you we were already in a scene and you'd already submitted?" She gave him a wink and leaned back in her seat.

Submission didn't always exist in a neat little box or behind closed doors. How often did the committed couples she'd seen at The Playroom prove the same? Some people only liked to conduct their play in private, but she'd watched men and women let go completely, allowing every decision to be made by their Dominant, down to clothing and food selections.

He frowned but didn't break visual contact. "I've been accommodating, as a gentleman should be. I'm not asking for a spanking or to be tied up."

"That's where we'll disagree. The things you've been doing are commands, not questions paired with fluttering lashes or coy looks. As for the tying and spanking, if you're interested in the act, you can let me know now." And instinct told her pain wouldn't work on this one. "But a lot of submissive work has nothing to do with sex or inflicting pain. It's about letting me in here." She leaned forward and put her index and middle finger flat against his forehead.

He inhaled sharply at the contact and let his fork hit the plate.

Laney knew this would be the moment of truth, and she needed to ask. Needed finality on whether this date had a longer shelf life than an hour in a restaurant. In truth, she should've been out at his initial resistance, but his use of "never" goaded her to push, to prod. Men in her dungeon stayed far away from such a word.

"Do you want me in here?" She poked him again.

He finally lifted his head, a determined, neutral expression on his face. "If you think you can handle it."

Chapter Three

This woman, his date, Lacey...a package he thought he'd figured out until she'd shown up and acted unlike the information he'd read. Tonight, he'd expected to be put in his place right away, to be directed and demeaned. But she'd acted caring, gentle, and disarming, even taken the time to learn how to say his name and to be open about herself. Then she'd coaxed him out of his natural shell, his need to retreat into the quiet and zone out of interaction.

Kanoa had never been more charmed in his life. A blonde, vivacious woman wearing a short denim skirt and jean vest. Sparkling pink Cupid's bow lips designed for kissing. He hadn't expected her hair to be down and flowing. The images he'd seen had her with a ponytail, reflecting a neat appearance. And then there came the mystery of her eyes, blue instead of green. He hadn't asked about contacts, figured it'd be rude, but the woman in the email Madame Eve sent never said anything about contacts, nor her affinity for boots with spurs. *Holy hell.* Those spurs jingled with every step and, now, the tip of her left foot tapped against the tile floor, clinking with each tap.

Throughout the whole conversation, he'd been absorbing her, not paying too much attention to her *commands*, as she called them, but more to her person, her body. Her fidgeting movements, and eagerness to touch him told him she liked what she saw and wanted him in ways he'd only been able to signify in one word...dirty.

"Did you ever give your commanding officers this much trouble?"

Boy, did I ever. "It took a few punishments to make me see reason." More than a few. He'd suffered public humiliation at times, scrubbing bathroom floors and toilets in his underwear or running a mile in snowstorm in the middle of the night. He'd never told anyone those reprimands made him appreciate those officers even more. They weren't willing to put up with his crap, and each commander worked damn hard to keep him on the straight and narrow.

"So, you're stubborn?"

"A bit. I don't believe respect should be given unless earned."

She smiled, a wide, Cheshire cat grin. "What does someone have to do to earn yours?"

Interesting question because most of the women he took to bed only cared about earning one thing from him, and the thing they wanted required multiple hours, plenty of effort, and repeat performances. "My closest friend earned my respect by calling me on my shit and then choosing to sludge through the mud, dirt, and cockroach-infested places we were shipped to with me as his partner. I guess other people have gotten it by not being like everyone else."

And by treating him like he was just another person, not anyone special, someone worth the same as them. Except, to get those words out of his mouth, he'd need to trust the person sitting across from him. Trust, like respect, became secured over time. So far, Kanoa followed his gut. This same instinct had saved lives on most of his military missions and was accurate more often than he wanted. Gut feeling told him Lacey hid something tonight, as for whether such a something would be a big deal...he'd stick around to find out.

"What about things like faith, being dependable?" The woman proved to be good at fishing, and their thoughts appeared to be aligned.

He tapped his fingers on the table. "If someone wants your respect, those things will naturally fall in line. At least in my experience that's how it goes, though I believe in different levels of reliance."

"Tell me about the levels." Leaning back, she crossed her legs and relaxed into the booth with a twinkle in her eye, as if the words he'd speak were some sort of fairy tale meant to amuse.

"All right, they are more like circles. My family and close friends are in the most intimate one. This circle is where I give them my heart, my life, and in return they'd trust me to protect theirs. The second is for those who I know, possibly intimately, and I'd offer my help as much as they'd offer theirs, with exceptions. My life is not for them. The last is for those I barely know, like the people I work with or meet at my job. I rely on those people as long as they give me no reason to doubt their sincerity toward my well-being. Threaten my safety and everything is up in the air." He'd functioned in a similar fashion for years. The process served him well and kept his emotions safe.

"If someone threatens your well-being, can they earn a spot back?"

A few had tried, but no one really wanted to. "I've found most people don't bother trying to get back. They are happier without me or my standards. What about you?"

She pushed her plate toward the center of the table and propped her elbows on the Formica tabletop. "In my line of work and hobbies, people trust me every day. I don't always give them the same amount of faith or all of me, but firmly believe they can rely on me as a caretaker. Ultimately, I want to give people a touchstone, someone they can count on when others may not be worthy of the same."

He found comfort in her statement. Her sheer poise, confidence in her strengths, and what she did for others served as testament to her character. There hadn't been a right time to tell her, but Lacey had already earned a spot of respect with him. In the midst of those thoughts, she stroked his skin again. Her index finger trailed along his hand, across the palm, until she rested hers in his.

"Would you give me a chance to earn your confidence?" Her question and the heat exuding from their contact sent a surge of lust through him. He wanted this. Badly. "Would you open yourself up to submission?"

Kanoa experienced a myriad of additional emotions over the next minute—fear, anxiousness, restlessness, and lust. He wanted to say yes and no. Both responses warred inside him, and so, instead of answering, he kept silent, bowed his head, and squeezed her hand.

She broke their connection and stood up, sliding out of the booth. "I'll tell you what. I'm going to head to the bathroom and, when I get back, you tell me if you're up to accepting my offer. If you're willing, then I'll treat you to dessert. If not, we go our separate ways."

He nodded in agreement, and she walked off. The way she'd said "dessert," her eyes flashing, lingered in his mind. The one word spoke volumes as to her intentions. If he said yes, there'd be no turning back from a submissive experience, unless he safed out— something he believed to be weak. Throughout all his watching, which he'd enjoyed a lot, no one had used their safeword. They took punishments and rewards with equal amounts of pleasure. He believed in doing the same. Now to decide if he had the courage to risk his first time with this woman, who was unlike the one he'd pictured.

***

Laney kept her cool until she got to bathroom. After splashing cold water on her face, she gazed at her reflection in the mirror. The same stare she'd given Kanoa appeared a lot less confident to her. Goose bumps pebbled her flesh at the thought of her date. He'd revealed a lot about himself and proved through his conversations he'd be a perfect candidate for sensory deprivation. The man begged to be deprived, to be limited, confessing those preferences through his stubborn attitude and military choices.

When the conversation drifted to his trust circles, she'd contemplated confessing who she was. Except her interest in him, in dominating him, had risen with each sentence. The idea of giving the opportunity up, potentially to her sister, stirred some agitated envy. No, she wanted a crack at this one herself. The only challenge would be performing the scene. She knew little about her sister's talents, since her sister never broadcasted her sessions to the club at large. Lacey believed her sessions to be sacred and enjoyed keeping them private.

She dug her cell phone out of her vest pocket and pressed the speed dial for her sister.

One ring and she picked up. "How'd it go?"

"Fine, everything is perfect. He's hotter than sex-on-a-stick and muscles, everywhere. I think he's rocking zero body fat. And he's loyal to his friends, rides a motorcycle—you are seriously missing out tonight, Lace."

"Well, that blows. Hold on." The sounds of rustling tissue and honking rattled through the phone. "I mean it blows in a completely literal sense."

"Sorry to hear you're still under the weather, Sis."

"If you're on your way, can you pick me up a can of chicken noodle soup and some cough drops?"

Laney felt awful because she didn't plan on coming home anytime soon. "I would if that were the case, but I called for another reason."

"Then what's up? Don't drag this out. Let the verbal diarrhea spill."

"Not the image I want in my head right now. But I'll give you a free pass because of the medicine. I need you to tell me how to conduct a sensory deprivation scene."

Her sister let out a strangled half laugh, half cough. "You're joking, right?"

Sure, her experiences were rooted in other kinks, but, like any kink, there were basics she could follow. "No, I'm serious."

"Those types of scenes I can't give simple phone directions for."

"What if you could see what was going on in the room and I could hear you? Take direction from you in real time?"

Lacey snorted. "You're crazy. How would you pull that off?"

If anyone else suggested to her what she was getting ready to say, she'd call them crazy, too. Except the more the idea turned over in her head, the more she believed they could pull it off. "I'd wear a Bluetooth set in the room and turn on the broadcast. You'd watch from the computer and direct me because you'd see everything via video and hear through the phone. I'd go audio silent on the broadcast, which would limit the number of people viewing." Experience had proven only the biggest voyeurs would watch a scene they couldn't hear. Typically, people wanted a full immersion from the comfort of their bedrooms.

"Is he okay with this?"

"I wouldn't tell him about the part of you being on the phone. I'd make him submit to the broadcast. Of course, I'd start it before he got in the room, but it'd be one of my requirements. It always has been." Every session, without fail, she let people watch. Privacy didn't make her hot. Knowing, even in the back of her mind, that other people were somewhere jerking off, playing with themselves as she played with someone else, got her wetter than any vanilla sex play ever had.

"I'm not sure I'm cool with this. Why are you willing to do this?"

Another question she'd been twirling back and forth like a baton between two hands, except she didn't have the best answer. "I just want to help him. If you'd been here.... Well, you wouldn't be doing the same thing, but I can see his pain. Feel it flowing through him, a constant he can't find release from. This is his release. I know it."

Her sister stayed silent for a minute, and Laney started to think Lacey would never agree. Then she said, "Tell me. Tell me how you know."

Chapter Four

She'd been gone for nearly twenty minutes, and Kanoa almost went to see if she had fallen into the toilet or something. Instead, he'd busied himself with cleaning up their dinner trash. The restaurant was big on self-service to help keep costs down. When he'd returned to stand by their table, she walked around the corner from the bathroom and headed for him.

"I apologize for taking so long. My sister called."

"Is everything all right?" He hoped this wouldn't put an end to their evening. Neither of them sat back down, and, as the moment unfurled, the air grew thick. So thick, he'd swear he'd been transported to the island in the humid summer.

She smiled, a half grin that didn't quite meet her eyes but gave him a bit of reassurance. "Nothing at all. She wanted to make sure everything was going okay and ask me to pick up a few things when I go home later. She's got a nasty bug, snuck up on her really."

"Are you sure you don't need to leave?"

"Well, I planned on leaving...with you."

The end of her sentence lingered as well. An open invitation he merely had to pluck from the air with open arms of acceptance. There were some unspoken invitations, too. No doubt involving a scene during which, he'd be expected to submit. To give her permission to call the shots. The only other time he'd allowed such a thing was in the military, allowing his superiors to control the what, where, who, and how he did things. The why, well, such a question fell beyond his pay grade.

"I'm up for dessert." He held a hand out to her, and she clasped his large, dark one with her small, slender, pale one. A perfect fit, and he loved how she radiated warmth and enjoyed being touched.

"Do you mind following me?" She asked the question with her head cocked to one side and a mischievous smirk.

"Not at all. Lead the way."

Fifteen minutes later, they pulled into an alley behind a string of brick buildings in downtown Rogers. He parked his bike behind her SUV and hopped off, tucking his keys into his pocket. The buildings were old, definitely early nineteenth century. They held a bit of mystery to them, contained secrets, and the adventurer in him came

101

crawling forth. He loved exploring old buildings, caves, anything with its own story.

"Like what you see?" Lacey's voice called out to him from the shadows near her vehicle.

"Not sure, but these old buildings are pretty awesome." "Good because we're going into one of those." She stepped up to him and looped an arm through his. "We'll enter through the front."

They took a leisurely stroll back the way they came and trailed the sidewalk around to the front entrance. A wooden sign hung above an elaborate set of double doors, calling out to the world in big, gold letters The Playroom. A bodyguard, bald and wearing all black leather, stood sentinel, determining who went in. He gave Kanoa a once-over, sizing him up, but when his gaze settled on the gorgeous woman beside him, the bastard grinned. Kanoa did his best, military best, to stomp the jealous tic winding its way into his belly. He wanted to slap the beaming smile right off the jerk's face but kept himself from acting on it.

"Hi, Ron. How's things?"

"A bit slow tonight, Pretty Woman. See you have a friend with you."

"He's new."

The bodyguard nodded and stepped aside. He called out after them, "Have a good time."

Overall, the club atmosphere gave him a down-home, country feel. A stage in the far right corner featured a round of karaoke singing. There were pool tables, a mechanical bull, and everything inside reflected a barn-house motif, contrasting the brick layers from the early 1900s outside the building.

He'd slowed to take in the scene, the people, and presence of the place, but Lacey dragged him forward, and he trod along with her until they came to a halt at the bar's edge.

"Garrett!" she yelled and slapped her hand on the bar's polished wood surface.

A man, probably mid-thirties, with a full beard and shaggy dark-blond hair, handed off two beers to a couple of patrons, wiped his hands on a towel, and walked toward them. As he got close, the grin on Garrett's face faded, replaced with confusion instead. "What are you doing here, Pretty Woman?"

"My sister caught a cold. Say hi to my date."

"Howdy," the bartender said with a nod aimed at him.

Kanoa returned the greeting. "Nice place."

"Thanks, I put a lot into it." He looked at Lacey next. "You're headed to the play area tonight?"

"My room," she replied.

"Play safe."

His date laughed and led the way to a door on the other side of the bar, one with a key code. She plugged in the numbers, and, when the pad lit up green, the lock clicked and the door swung open.

"Are you sure you want to do this?" Her question came coupled with her teeth biting down on her lower lip.

He doubted this would be his last chance to back out, since the entire D/s world existed and thrived on being consensual. This woman added an additional layer of ensuring agreement and he appreciated it. "Yes."

"All right, follow me. To my dungeon."

Laney had never been so nervous in her life. Thankfully, Ron and Garrett didn't question who her date was and why she'd brought someone they'd never met to the club. Definitely not her usual modus operandi, and typically she played with other members of The Playroom, keeping her interactions to those already vetted. The fact both doorman and establishment owner called her by her handle meant they knew she wasn't her sister.

Too late to worry about repercussions now, especially since the guy she wanted alone followed her down a flight of stairs into The Playroom basement. What hid down in the dark was the true purpose to the club, a place where kinky folks who enjoyed their own proclivities could get it on without fear of being found out. She and Lacey had special ties to Garrett, so, thankfully, they didn't pay quite the fee others did to rent dungeons. The only downside was they shared.

They walked slowly down the carpet-covered stairs, white rope lights illuminating the edges. When they came to the bottom, she went left, back underneath the staircase to where their room and the owner's were nestled. Back away from the others, separated, and slightly larger. They had quite a collection of toys as well as a private bathroom preparation area shared between the two spaces.

She snagged the keycard from the back pocket of her jean skirt and swiped it on the keycard lock. A beep and the door opened.

"You have some sophisticated security." Kanoa's voice vibrated through her, a deep sound reawakening her desire all over again.

"Doing what we do, it's all about safety first. For us, for our guests." She strutted into the room and turned the dial on the wall, bathing everything in low light. "Shut the door behind you."

Once she heard the latch catch, she swiveled, following her date's gaze as it trailed around the furnishings. "See anything you like?"

He cleared his throat. "Several things."

"Tell me."

"The bed looks pretty magnificent, and I like the St. Andrew's cross." He paused, eyes stopping on her prize. "The saddle. What do you do there?"

"You can do a lot of things. Before we get started, let's talk rules, limits. There's the club standard, no rape play, knife play, or strangulation play. My other limits include no topping from bottom, you must use your safeword to stop all play, and the entire session is broadcast on a live video feed. No exceptions."

He didn't seem happy with the last rule she presented, and he crossed his arms while sharply exhaling. "Why the video?"

"Because of your fear to be seen as weak. This is the ultimate test, to show others you can submit, and it is not a weakness. It makes you powerful. Those watching are either too afraid to come here themselves or will be envious you are submitting to me and not to them. Do you agree?"

Kanoa released his defensive posture and nodded. "I agree."

She pointed to the door on the left wall. "Go through there and strip. Put on a pair of the white boxers from the shelf and then return. Use this time to prepare, use the facilities, and when you walk out, I will ask you your safeword. Then we begin."

"I look forward to it," he replied with a smirk then followed her instructions.

As soon as he disappeared and the lock engaged, she called her sister. Three rings and then finally a pickup. "Took you guys a bit. I almost went to sleep."

"Do you have your laptop ready?"

"Yes, yes. It's ready. Turn the broadcast on."

Laney walked to the light switch and flipped the toggle next to the strip of tape labeled vid. "I'm going to put you on speaker, and, after I get the noise-cancelling headphones and the blindfold on, I'll put in the Bluetooth."

"All right. What is he interested in?" Her sister's question came with a cough and, for a split second, the nervous guilt she still possessed at the idea of acting out this mad idea doubled. She should let Lacey rest, but, instead, recruited her.

"You know what? Let's just cancel."

"What the hell are you talking about?"

"Lace, you're sick, and I shouldn't even be—"

"No, no, no. You are not changing your mind on me. You look hot as hell in your outfit. The viewers' numbers are already ticking upward in anticipation. When your sub walks out of the prep room, let's just say I won't let you disappoint him. He needs this. That's what you said. We're performing a service, so quit thinking otherwise."

Laney shook her head. "Fine. He needs to be forced to submit, to be deprived. He expressed interest in the St. Andrew's cross and the bed. But his favorite was my saddle bench."

"Everyone's a sucker for the cowboy getup."

"Yes, but my usual performances are me solo with a bunch of people watching, restraining a guy.... This guy on my saddle, it's new." The fantasy already had her panties soaked. Most men kept to the basics, and not once had she ever put a man in her saddle.

"He'll be marvelous. Now, sister, put your Bluetooth in, and I think the big thing will be to get his eyes covered. Let's proceed slowly, but, if his eyes are covered, he'll never know you're talking to me. I'll walk you through some basic motions. The biggest thing will be not to push him too hard. You said this is his first time participating in a scene. They are typically easier to break as virgins."

Laney turned on the little earpiece, and the blue light blinked twice to signal a connection. The door to the prep area opened as she swept her hair back into place to cover her ear. When she pivoted to face him, her mouth went dry and her eyes wide. He stood in nothing but the white boxers all her male subs wore, except where the boxers were intended to be the only adornment on a sub's body, his revealed tons of tattoos. Some people talked about getting sleeves, tats running the length of an arm or part of one. Kanoa's body art resembled a T-shirt, spanning from the lower deltoid to cover his entire chest. Did it wrap around to his back, too? There were dozens of images, a sun, a moon, a turtle, waves, and so much more. The symbols and pictures told a story, one inspired to make the viewer ask questions or to create their own stories.

Clearing her throat, she worked her way past the momentary attraction to ask, "Safeword?"

"U'i wahine." He stepped into the room and shut the door, closing them off once more, securing their place and his confidence in joining in the scene.

"This is the last time you'll use the word unless you want to end the scene. Do you understand?"

He nodded, interlocking his hands in front of his waist. Such long arms, and, damn, those tats should've encircled all the skin to his wrists.

"Verbalize your understanding."

"I won't use the word unless I want to end our scene early."

"Good." Lacey's voice echoed in her ear. "Get the blindfold. And while you approach to secure it, you're going to ask him a series of questions."

She grabbed the leather, padded blindfold and smiled. "Now, get on your knees."

He dropped with ease.

"I will approach and put this blindfold in place. I'm also going to ask you a series of questions. It's important to be completely honest because your answers will determine how this scene will operate. If you do not tell me how you really feel, it will affect the level of pleasure you'll get from this session. Reply 'Yes, Pretty Woman,' if you understand and agree."

Kanoa looked the tasty supplicant on his knees, head and back straight, hands still interlocked, and resolute gaze focused on her. A tried and true soldier. "Yes, Pretty Woman."

"All right. Ask the following...."

She exhaled slowly, listening to her sister recite the first two questions then she delivered the lines. "Do you like pain?"

"I do, but my tolerance is too high. I've yet to find someone who can inflict pain on me that will surpass what I'm used to."

Laney took a step forward. "Name two fantasies you have about a scene."

"Being told what to do or how to act without having to think, and to be restrained."

Interesting, since restraint sat at the top of the list, but the idea seemed too tame. "Are you claustrophobic?"

"No."

She reached him and trailed five fingers up his arm, letting her nails score the skin. Not too deep but enough to enjoy seeing gooseflesh pebble up. "Any other fears?"

"My only fear is to lose my family."

"Any other things you don't want me to do to you?" Placing the blindfold over his eyes, she drew the ties back around his head, tying a simple bow knot in place. The blood pounded in her ears. This experience affected her in a way she hadn't expected. Normally, her sessions were sex based, but this would be everything except the act.

"I'm up for anything within house rules, Pretty Woman." His voice washed over her like water on her body, sensitizing her to him and granting her visions of him hovering over her, pounding inside or letting her ride him to orgasm oblivion.

"Tell him to stand and walk twenty paces forward." Lacey's voice broke her out of her momentary daydream.

"Stand and walk twenty steps forward." She followed him and loved how he took sure, quick steps. No fear, no doubt. A good sign. "Now, turn ninety degrees to your left and bend over the saddle bench."

He put his hands out and found the pommel then bent his body over the leather and wood contraption. This bench, designed to be longer than a traditional horse saddle, could be used for sex and restraint in half a dozen positions. She planned to put him in an extremely vulnerable one. No direction from Lacey, this next part came from her. All instinct.

"Rotate your body so your face is next to the pommel on one side and straddle the seat."

He did as requested.

"Hold the position for five minutes. During these five minutes, you cannot speak, move, or make any noise no matter what happens. If you do, I will add an additional five minutes to the time. Nod to show me you understand."

Kanoa nodded. His tats covered only the upper part of his back. Glorious and on display for her perusal. She took a moment to look over more images, tribal bands, and countless little pieces merging into one large work of art.

"Good. Five minutes starts now."

Her sister spoke in her ear. *"Light a candle. We'll play with temperature sensations first. He's not restrained, and this will test his resolve."*

Laney hesitated. Typically, she'd save things like this for people who'd been doing scenes for a while. Her method would have been to use a flogger and increase to a cane.

"Don't hesitate or worry. Trust me, this guy is trained to take this. What you have to do is provide something unexpected. He'll expect floggers and whips. Light the damn candle."

She grabbed a lighter and put flame to the taper wick. Less than a minute later, she stood ready. No words, just following instructions, she let wax fall onto the small of his back and started a trail from the bottom of his spine to the dip between his shoulder blades.

"Three minutes left. Lift one foot at a time and drop wax in the center of each sole. Then have him hold each foot in the air."

Kanoa remained stoic through the process. When she lifted each leg by the calf and unleashed the wax droplets in the center of each foot, he almost moved. His determination to fight against the urge, no doubt with gritted teeth, impressed her. Once both appendages had been treated and left dangling in the air, she followed Lacey's next bit of torture, scraping the wax off with a steel cuticle pusher.

The little tool left behind a small sting and proved effective for prolonging the experience.

This action produced better results, and once she thought he flinched. The skin underneath each coin of wax was red and irritated, like she wanted it to be. The last ones, though, she drew out, letting the pusher move slowly. Wanting, no, longing for him to cry out or to react.

"Interesting." Her sister sounded as amazed as she was by his strength.

"Time's up. Now, turn onto your back, wrap your hands around the pommel, and cross your legs to elevate them onto the saddle."

Again, he followed the instructions without fail, like he'd trained to do this his whole life. Like he wanted to do it. Once he assumed the position, she asked, "Are you ready to continue?"

"Yes, Pretty Woman. I can handle more."

She chuckled. "Confident, are we?"

"No." He grinned, the blindfold unfortunately hiding the smile she knew lurked in his eyes. The same facial expression had been granted to her at the restaurant, and, for a split second, she wished the scene was done and she had a chance to get him intimately to herself. "Determined to win."

"Then let us begin anew." She'd work with Lacey to make sure this man knew subspace before the scene ended or she'd break him trying to get him there.

Chapter Five

Kanoa was ready for another round of wax. Honestly, he'd been surprised by her tactic, expecting a barrage from a flogger. Instead, she'd turned to something he hadn't expected. When she let the wax drip onto his back, he'd believed she'd never get him to react. Until his feet. Holy hell, his restraint to stay still got tested there, especially when she removed the wax.

Somehow, in blindfolding him, she created a connection between his body and hers. Her body heat radiated against him whenever she got near. When she left his proximity, his body ran cold.

He expected her to do more wax play. Instead, she moved away. Minutes ticked by. He struggled to hear the slightest shuffle or jingle, except maybe she'd slipped off her boots or stopped moving entirely. His heart thumped, blood pumping rapidly through his body and drowning out the other noises in the room he'd picked up on. The hum of the air conditioner, the ticking of a clock—all gone, leaving him with nothing but his anxious need to move. To do something. Only the fear she'd end everything if he moved kept him in place.

Finally, he couldn't take any more. "Pretty Woman, are you still here?"

A low laugh echoed from across the room. "You don't like being left in the dark, do you, Kanoa?"

He cursed under his breath. Everything about this room, this scene, this woman seemed to be a never-ending test. "I wanted to make sure you didn't leave me." Honesty helped in all situations.

"You should trust in our mutual pleasure occurring from us occupying the same room. Now, what shall your punishment be?"

"Name it and I will do it, Pretty Woman." How he wanted it to involve worshipping her. To touch her, even. The waiting sent him to new heights of torture.

She approached him, crouching on his left side. Whispering in his ear, she said, "I want you to be silent and taste what you do to me."

A small rustling noise occurred next, followed by her fingers at his mouth. He opened, ready to suck only to have a soaked, delicious-smelling thong shoved inside. He closed around it, let the aroma and taste of her overwhelm him. In the same second, a cold, stinging pain about the size of a golf ball assailed him and began a path from his neck down across his chest. Slow, agonizing, and he didn't dare cry out, afraid she'd take the gag out, that she'd stop.

Everything she did came as a surprise, as unexpected. This is what he wanted—someone to give and take, to be different as well.

Another ball joined the first, twin spheres, freezing and acute. She guided them on a path down his chest, letting them sit on his belly, balanced by his position on the bench.

"I'll have my underwear back, please." She snatched the thong out of his mouth, leaving him with his jaw hanging open and panting. He couldn't see, only heard a click as she picked up the two spheres. More agonizing seconds ticked by then a cold hand snaked underneath his boxers and traced the edges of the elastic.

"Can you handle more?"

"Yes, Pretty Woman." He had no clue what *more* entailed, but he longed for the torture, for her to touch his stiff cock. His arousal turned more painful as she yanked his boxers down, exposing him. In the back of his mind, the reminder of how others could see, that he'd been exposed, took over. He wanted to ask her to stop, to call out the safeword and cover himself. Yet, the idea of not seeing how this would end killed him. He could handle this if she could.

He jerked as a piece of moist fabric was wrapped around his cock, securing the ice-cold balls against the base, touching both scrotum and shaft. Instead of shrinking at the sensation, he got harder.

"I'm going to secure you to the bench now. Do you have a preference on restraints?"

"No. Use what you'd like."

She tutted at him. "Naughty, naughty. This night isn't about my pleasure. It's about yours. What should I use?"

"Ropes are fine." He really didn't care, just wanted her hands on him again. To feel the heat of her fingers around his shaft once more. Damn. He'd sell his soul.

"Your wish is my command. I will bind you, but, as punishment, you have to pick your favorite year. Two digits only."

His mind searched frantically to recall the year he entered the military. By far, the date stood out as the single most important time to him. "O-eight, the best one by far."

"Tell me why." She began with his wrists, using an abrasive rope to loop around and between his flesh and the pommel. Two then three loops around each one.

"It's when I entered the service. That time of my life was by far the best, the most fulfilling. I had to prove myself physically, intellectually. No skating by because of my body type or success with sports or the ability to attract women. I worked hard to earn respect and rank. It started at boot camp and continued for six years."

During the time he'd rambled, she'd secured his legs, binding his ankles to the side supports of the bench. Never, not even in boot, had he been so thoroughly exposed.

"Thank you for telling me about those memories. Now, you'll remain silent, and, for the next eight minutes, only instruments of my choosing will touch your flesh."

"Yes, Pretty Woman." The word she'd used, "instruments" could mean a million and one things, and, since the start of the scene, he'd learned anything could happen. So far, she'd proved to be unlike her profile. Beneath the surface, this woman possessed depths he found he wanted more than anything the lines of text had presented to him.

A whip crack brought his thoughts back to the present. Then the same sound happened again, along with a sting against his skin. The subsequent strikes honed the pain into narrow points. Like a master, she nailed him in the same spots across his pectorals without fail. As the minutes passed, the edge of each of the whip's tails became like stinging needles. The sound of crickets buzzed in his ears, his mouth dried, and he bit hard enough on his lip to break skin.

Then she stopped, only to snap a thin reed against his calves. Up and down, the saddle arrangement leaving him exposed as she peppered the front and the back. Relentless and unforgiving, she moved to his thighs. Finally, she reached his sac. Two snaps and he let go. His muscles went limp, no longer able to tense. His body felt weightless, as though he floated. The pain dulled into this force sustaining him on some plane he'd never inhabited before.

Euphoria had him asking, "More, please."

Her breath hitched when Kanoa cried out. She needed to see his eyes, his full facial expression. The only reason he'd be asking for more was because he'd reached subspace. Had to have.

"Don't stop now. Keep going."

"I have to take the blindfold off." She'd spoken to her sister, aloud, but she'd spoken without thought. She snapped the reed on his hips, trailing a path upward and listening to his pants. Short, staccato breaths and his rock-hard, twitching cock proved she'd found the sweet spot. Her endorphins soared at an all-time high, but the icing on the cake would be to take in his glazed-over eyes.

She yanked the blindfold upward, and his eyes shot open. Hazy, glossed, he attempted to focus on her, so she snapped the bamboo reed against one armpit then the other. Next were the spots next to his clavicle. Finally, she tapped against his jugular. Those pressure points were killers, and each action got her a moan, at first soft then louder. The last moan a drawn out groan coupled with, "Please."

"Bye." She clicked off the Bluetooth and yanked it out of her ear, dropping it to the floor. His one-word plea spoke to action. He needed it. She needed it. Except she wouldn't fuck him with an audience. No, they'd have to settle for oral.

Laney chose to straddle him, hiking her skirt up, and planting her clean-shaven vagina on his mouth. "Feast," she demanded, and he followed her direction.

He tongued her from hood to the bottom of her opening. Delicious, single-minded, insane focus on pleasuring her. So, she set out to distract him, leaning forward to let the fabric of her clothes brush against his already-sensitized skin. Then she wrapped one hand around his shaft and tugged roughly. He growled against her already-soaked and heated flesh. The vibrating sound rattled up her spine, arousing—further proof he liked things rough.

His attentions turned ravenous, as if he were wild and untamed. The entire time she teased him with her hands, the pressure built. Her mouth stayed uninvolved. Instead, fingers roved, caressed, jerked, and flicked, heightening or lessening his ministrations, depending on the action. She learned what he liked, how he liked it, and all the while she careened toward release.

When her orgasm finally took over, she embraced the tingling sensation cascading over her body. Let the release wash over her in finality. She lost control and let the pleasure consume her—orgasms tended to drive her out of her mind. After she came back down from the momentary high, Kanoa gave her a long lick, like the first one he'd applied, and she eased off of him.

She'd already decided what she'd do next. But, first, the video broadcast needed to be switched off. She wanted this moment to be between them, and them alone. She didn't like the idea of sharing this sexual moment with anyone else. So she flipped the switch on the wall and came back to her sub, still secured to his bench. He watched her, too, the keen intelligence in his eyes honed on her every move, his arousal still evident. No doubt, if she didn't utter these next words, he'd want to take advantage of the big bed in the corner.

Nervous and unsure how to word the next verbal command, she stopped short of completely reaching him.

"What's wrong, Lacey?"

She'd given herself away, obviously, and the name he'd uttered outlined the problem exactly. "I confess, I'm not Lacey."

"U'i wahine."

She'd expected him to safe out. So, she went and untied him, released him from his arm bonds, and then stepped back, providing the distance for him to finish the process. In her whole time as a Domme she'd never had a sub use their safeword until now. Except, this particular situation called for it, and the guilt overwhelmed. Truth be told, her guilt had grown ten times since she'd last checked. Most likely because they'd taken the scene into the physical-connection side of things. She'd planned on keeping it 100 percent nonsexual. Yet, his begging and his submission caused her to do some crazy-ass things.

Now, she'd earned his censure and violated his trust.

He said nothing as he got up from the saddle bench and stalked to the preparation room. He'd closed himself off from her, shutting her out, like he'd promised he'd do to anyone who tried to hurt him. She'd no doubt caused more harm than good. His first submissive experience involved being misled.

Once the door shut, she started the process of putting the room to rights. Cleaning the equipment, dropping the golf balls into the cleaning solution, positioning the reed back in the display, and coiling the ropes together once more. The tedious tasks did nothing to keep her from wondering what would happen if she barged into the preparation room and confessed the rest, told the story. No doubt he wouldn't want to hear it, but those words needed to be said. Her soul necessitated a cleansing by truth telling. *Truth sets you free* or some such thing had to be a famous quote somewhere.

She readjusted her clothing, put her boots back on, and headed for the door. Before she reached it, the damn thing swung open, and Kanoa stood there, neutral expression intact.

He didn't move, merely stared her down, and she had to speak. "I'm sorry for not telling you who I was from the start. I just—"

"Then who are you?" No censure, no inflection, merely a question.

"My name is Laney, and I'm Lacey's twin."

"I figured as much. What was so horrible about me that my date couldn't meet me?" Anger edged his words.

"She got a cold, a bad one. But she thought I could keep you company, and, to be honest, I didn't expect things to go this far. Didn't expect to like you so much or want to help you. I need to confess one other thing. I had Lacey on a Bluetooth, helping me through our session. I'm not an expert at your kink, not by far, and success is important to me. I did this for you, although seeing you come apart was a bit on the selfish side. But you have to believe me, I—"

"Enough." The word came out low, on a growl.

She stood there, hands clasped, afraid he'd walk out of this room and they'd never talk again. Some would be afraid of Kanoa due to his size. He could easily overpower her, but she didn't fear his strength. She feared his censure. He'd awoken some need in her for closeness, and the session had rocked her world as much as his. There was something to be said for sharing a side of yourself with only one companion.

"Thank you for your help and good night."

Her chest tightened, but she kept it together as he walked past her and slammed the dungeon door behind him. Once he left, she broke. Moisture welled in her eyes and she dropped to the floor. Her cell phone buzzed from across the room, but she couldn't drag herself up to get it. Didn't want to. Sometime during their date and session, she'd allowed herself to open up, to care too much. Like she tended to do with her therapy patients.

This would leave a bigger hole.

Chapter Six

Kanoa stalked up the stairs. Rage boiled in his blood. He wanted to storm back through the door, take his girl.... No, not his, but the dominant, maddening woman he'd left there. She'd tumbled him like a tower of bricks with the load-bearing ones carefully removed. Played him like a well-strung ukulele. Except, he became the fool so desperate to march to her beat, hoping and praying she'd have the solutions to calm him. Calm him she did. *Fuck.*

The signs had all been there, too. From the wrong nickname, Pretty Woman never being mentioned in the email he received. No, Lacey was called the Ice Queen. Add in the whispered "bye" she'd uttered midscene—he'd thought it a good-bye to keeping the scene sans intimacy; in fact, she'd hung up on her sister.

Once upstairs, he detoured to the polished wooden bar, which gave off a distinctive pine smell mixed with booze. Hell, he needed a drink, something to flush his system because he could still smell her. Her floral scent permeated his very being, cutting through his anger and reminding him of how she'd helped him. But even being upset over how she'd hidden things from him, he didn't feel restless like he normally did.

Sliding onto the bar stool, he signaled to Garrett. "What can I get you?"

"Jameson, double, on the rocks."

"Sounds like your trip downstairs didn't turn out as planned." The bartender moved away before he could respond.

The other people inside became background noise, a buzzing as he zoned out, remembering said "trip downstairs." From Laney's initial methods, to the more cutting ones, and even her final offer to allow him a chance to bring her to pleasure. *Damn.*

"Here ya go," Garrett called out.

The ice tinkled as the glass slid to a stop against his open palm. He lifted and drank deep, swallowing half of the whiskey without a second thought. The smoky char taste and the burn searing its way down his throat washed away the taste of *her* arousal. "Thank you."

"What did she do?"

The question caught him by surprise.

Normally, Kanoa kept his thoughts to himself. The only people he shared them regularly with were his therapist and maybe his boss, Sig. Trespasses were never spoken of, yet this bar owner possibly knew more about Laney than he ever would. So, why not? "All the right things until I found out she wasn't who she pretended to be."

A half smile appeared on the tender's face. "Wasn't she?"

"What the hell are you talking about?" A jealous flame lit inside him. How did this man even begin to understand what happened downstairs? Had he watched?

The bartender shook his head and leaned closer. "I won't pretend to know all the details, but I get a lot of folks in here searching for someone to relieve them of their pain. They aren't seeking honesty or truth, but a way to silence the building storm inside them. The people I've rented out those downstairs rooms to provide the answer. Personal information and facts are usually cast to the wayside. Now, I get it. You're the type who wants everyone to be straightforward because you hold yourself to such a high standard. But, if she'd been honest with you, would you have trusted your pain to her? You expected someone else, planned on someone else, right?"

Kanoa nodded, the suspicion and jealousy in him dying a little. Instead, an image of her face when they'd met in the restaurant flashed in his mind's eye. Her hesitance and smile compared to the serious picture of her sister.

"She wasn't what you planned, but she got you results."

"Yes, and made a fool out of me in the process." But Garrett's words hit home. He'd wanted someone to help him, someone to be a friend, and she'd met those requirements. Her little fib kept him on the date. If he'd found out the truth, he might have had more reservations, less trust, or even called it quits after dinner.

"We're all fools at some point or another. I'm sure she feels like one now." Garrett grabbed the bottle of Jameson and filled his glass once more. "I can tell you this. I've known Pretty Woman since college. She is one of the most caring and helpful people I've met, more than her twin. She'll punish herself for this error more than you ever could. I'll also say she doesn't bring just anyone back here, who isn't already a member. So, you"—he pointed a finger at him—"must be someone special."

Kanoa kicked back the rest of his drink and slapped a twenty on the bar top.

"Keep it. Drinks are on the house, tonight. Speaking of coincidence, look who just came to the main room."

The bartender's words got his head turning toward the hallway entrance. There she stood. Laney, her back straight, eyes sad, headed for the exit.

"Thanks, friend. Maybe I'll see you around." He stood and moved through the crowd, headed straight for his target. She moved fast for a woman a lot smaller than him, able to squeeze between couples while he had to ask them to move out of his way. Finally, he gave up and shouted her name, "Laney."

She stopped and scanned over her shoulder. Her gaze fell on him; he mouthed to her to wait for him. Thankfully, she got the message and stepped to the side. When he caught up to her, the nerves caught up to him. Even with everything that had transpired over the last few hours, this new meeting made him more nervous than being naked and strapped to her bench.

"What's up?" Her question came out indifferent, almost fearful— exactly what he didn't want.

"I think I owe you dessert this round."

She eyed him warily. "Is this a joke?"

"No joke. Thanks to your bartender friend—he made me realize I may have jumped the gun."

"Are you kidding me? I lied to you, kept things from you. You're not jumping anything. In fact, I deserve it."

He chuckled. "Do you trust me?"

"Yes."

"Then let's talk about it more somewhere else." He wanted her alone, in his hotel room. Without a video camera watching them or random people casting curious glances. No, they needed a private conversation.

"Do I follow you?"

He shook his head and grabbed her hand. "No, you ride with me. Your friend won't tow your Jeep, right?"

"No, he won't." She smiled. "You're serious?"

"As serious as a spotter dictating wind speed."

Reaching out, she put a hand in his. "Then let's go."

***

As they traveled the streets of Rogers, winding around curves and racing through stoplights, she was thankful for Kanoa's helmet. Without it, her hair would've been a rat's nest by the time they got to the Isle of Bermuda Hotel. She'd hesitated only a moment after getting on his bike. Wondering if she'd lost what little sense she possessed, agreeing to come here with him. Yet, she trusted him with her safety and believed in his honest desire to talk.

117

They walked through the lobby, the space decked out in tropical colors, palm trees, and a waterfall off to one side. Small groups of people milled around a lounge area in the middle of the room, drinking, laughing, and lost in their evening.

When they got on the elevator, the ride brought renewed silence, but they kept their hands linked. For some reason, touching him had become a necessity. As if breaking the connection might shatter the peace they'd begun to broker.

When they finally got to the room, he wrapped an arm around her waist and ushered her inside. Electric tapers illuminated a room awash in rose petals, jazz music playing in the background. "Um, Kanoa...."

"Oh, hell. I'm sorry, Laney. Give me just a minute." He scooted past her and flipped on the switch for the lamps. There was no helping the rose petals, but he put an end to the candles and the music swiftly.

She giggled. "Expecting a different end to your evening?"

"More like a pair of meddling friends who thought I needed assistance in the romance department."

"You're right. I think there may be a difference of opinion on what's romantic. At least they got the beverage right." Two glasses and a bottle of champagne on ice sat near a love seat.

"Would you like some?" His question held curiosity.

"I normally would, but let's talk first. Like you mentioned before we left The Playroom." She sat on the love seat and waited for him to join her. He paced first and then finally plopped onto a spot beside her. He popped the knuckles in both hands and rolled his shoulders, leaning back and then moving forward to prop his elbows on his thighs.

"What's wrong?"

"I'm not sure how to do this."

She sighed. "Do what? Talk? We did this earlier."

"No." He rotated to face her and made eye contact. "I want to kiss you."

Her chest tightened, the breath knocked out of her lungs. She hadn't given anyone a kiss since she'd broken up with her boyfriend over four years prior. "I don't really do such a thing."

"I didn't figure you did, but why not?"

He prized honesty, so she'd give him this to make up for her lies. "The last guy I kissed I'd planned on marrying. But he didn't like my kinks, couldn't understand why I wanted more. At first, I hid those things from him. When we finally talked about it, he considered me sick."

"You like tying guys up. I'm a guy who enjoys being tied up." Kanoa shrugged then sat back, draping one arm behind her along the back of the couch.

The idea he liked what they'd done made her heart flutter and a blush rise on her cheeks. He stated the whole concept as if it happened all the time, a perfectly normal thing.

"The truth, is I'm a voyeur and an exhibitionist. I like to watch and be watched. Sure, I don't mind tying someone down, administering punishment, but tonight, with you.... It's the first time I've enjoyed it." She caught his eyes, those deep browns burrowing into hers. Looking away, she gathered up the courage to continue her own confession. "Anyways, after the guy and I were over, I equated kissing with a relationship and most of the people I interacted with in my dungeon were not people I wanted to get involved with on a deeper level. So, I just didn't engage in such a way." Except she wanted to with him, wanted to connect with him in ways she'd not allowed herself in a long time.

His arm moved down a few inches and rested on her shoulder, tracing a pattern with his fingertips along her collarbone. "If I said I do, wanted to, would you let me?"

Gooseflesh pebbled on her arms at his ministrations. "You don't give up easily, do you?"

"Not when my instincts tell me this is one way to get the truth from you." He leaned in, and, at the same time, pulled her toward him.

She whispered, "What truth?"

"This one." His lips, mere inches from hers, were on a collision course. The heat expanded between them as the moment slowed to a crawl, the scent of whiskey teasing her nostrils. She breathed deep, bracing for impact, willing herself to be calm, unflappable...but then he kissed her.

Chapter Seven

He'd hoped she'd embrace the kiss and, with it, him. He didn't expect her tongue to be the first to reach out. Yet, she made the initial move to deepen their connection and surprised the hell out of him. Funny part was, she'd been doing the same thing all night. Laney, not Lacey, being the one to give new experiences, ones he'd enjoyed a bit too much.

So he opened himself to her and joined in equal exploration. Her hands came up to tangle with his hair, sliding along his scalp, and raising goose bumps on his arms. He loved it when she took control, directed him to bring them both pleasure. He'd been searching for this, someone to guide and take the reins. His gut said yes where his brain doubted. She'd hidden things and made him want more than ever before.

She dragged her palms down to his shoulders and pushed. He followed her lead, leaning back onto the couch with her resting on top. He went from barely registering to hard as a rock in less than a second. Anxiously hoping those magic palms would find their way to the southern hemisphere of his body. The kissing continued, slow, drugging, and emotionally charged meetings of tongue and lips. Her scent filled his nostrils, and he closed his eyes, immediately picturing this woman in his bed—not just tonight, but every night.

When she finally pulled back, they were both panting. "I haven't done that in—"

"Forever." He finished for her, and swiped a lock of her hair out of her face.

"Yes. Wait...you haven't?"

"No, I've been kissed with every escapade I've had, but those kisses didn't get me like this." He grabbed one of her hands and guided it down to the tent in his pants, pressing her against his erection.

"Oh, well." She blushed and ducked her head.

He couldn't tell if she was embarrassed or hesitant to take things further. So he decided to goad her instead. "Are you turning shy on me now?"

Her head snapped up, eyes flashing with challenge. "You forget yourself. When I climb off you, you will go to the bedroom, strip, and wait for me." She gave him a squeeze, not gentle in the least, and he naturally pulsed against her grip in anticipation.

Damn. She'd elevated this extremely fast, and he was ready. Had been ready since their scene, and, if she squeezed him again, he might end the fun before it even officially started. "Yes, Pretty Woman."

Laney scooted to the other side of the couch, putting plenty of distance between them. He didn't like the space. No, they should be close. If the only way to get her there involved following directions, so be it.

He pushed off the couch, took one last look at her, and went into the bedroom portion of the suite. It was also covered in rose petals. When this night wrapped up, he'd be giving Sig a few strong words about interfering in his personal interactions. He took a couple of minutes to grab the small trash can tucked in the corner of the room and swept the offending petals off the bed into their new home. Then he got back to the task Laney had given him.

Reaching one hand behind his head, he pulled off his shirt, shrugged out of his shoes, and shucked his jeans. She'd said naked, and he didn't want to prolong getting to the main event. He wanted nothing between them and sex...not a scene. The boxers went along with his socks, and he took the extra moments to fold the clothes and set them in one of the chairs near the window.

When he saw Laney in the doorway, watching him, her neutral expression made him self-conscious, and he struggled to maintain eye contact. Doubt was one emotion he didn't want, much less need. "Do I please you?"

"Yes, very much." She stepped into the room, unclasping the buttons on her denim vest. "But why do you only have tattoos on the entire front of your body and only part of the back? And what do all the different symbols mean?"

The fact she'd noticed sent a thrill through him. Most women only glanced at the tattoos, thinking they made him dangerous or tough. Rarely did they peer closer. "The tattoos are a tribal tradition and tell the story of my family and my life...my achievements. In all, it would take hours to discuss every line or image. As for my back, that's for the part of my life I've yet to live."

"What would you tattoo on your body to represent me?" She assumed a lot, but he hoped her question meant she'd already started feeling the same things he experienced.

"The shell symbol means I'm a warrior. I got this after serving in the Iraqi war. I would tattoo a turtle inside it as a symbol for peace, right here." He pointed to the top of his shoulder.

She tossed the vest and her shirt on top of his clothes, coming closer and giving him a view of her breasts—creamy, pale flesh covered in a pink lace bra. "You think so highly of me, even after what I did?"

So many questions, but he'd answer each one truthfully. "I didn't want to. But condemnation is hard to hang onto when your deceptions showed me things I'd never experienced, things I enjoyed."

She removed her boots. Then she shook her hips, sending the skirt sliding down those gorgeous legs of hers, pooling at her feet. A slow striptease from hell. His cock jerked at the lack of attention and the revelation she wore nothing under the skirt, never having bothered to replace the thong she'd stuffed in his mouth earlier. Clean-shaven, her lips were swollen and pink. He nearly moaned aloud.

"I'm glad you're willing to give this a chance, to give us a chance. Now there's nothing to stop us from feeling one another." She closed the distance between them, wrapping her arms around his neck, and standing on her tiptoes to peck his lips. Then she whispered, "Unclasp my bra."

He followed her request, and, once the metal clips sprung from their homes, she discarded it with her other clothing. When the hard tips of her nipples touched his lower chest, he shuddered. Then she guided his hand to her warm heat. He traced her clit with two fingers, watching her eyes go wide as he parted her lips and slowly inserted two digits, her reaction alone well worth slow movement, as she moaned, "Kanoa."

"Tell me, Pretty Woman. Command me."

Her head fell back, and he moved his free arm to support her as she rode his fingers, and ground against him. "Keep this up until I come."

In return for his attentions, she grabbed his erection and stroked in an equally rough, tugging motion. Similar to the one she'd employed in her dungeon. He tensed as her inner walls gripped his fingers and her body began to shudder. Somehow, through her release, even as her legs locked, she told him, "Don't come."

Her masterful stroking stopped as her orgasm crested, and, when she finally came down, he removed his hand and sucked the remnants of her release into his mouth. "You taste delicious."

"And you do, too." She dropped to her knees. "I've wanted to put you in my mouth since I had you strapped to my saddle." She inhaled his length as if it were a Popsicle on the verge of melting. Her focus and determination to make him lose his self-control continued until he tensed as she had, and it took every ounce of willpower to not grab the back of her head. Yet, she wanted him to, reaching for a hand and encouraging him to wrap her long hair around it. He used it as an anchor to keep himself from falling backward. All too quickly, blood pounded in his ears, his toes curled, and he cried out as his orgasm attacked, spurting into her mouth. She licked and sucked up every last drop.

When she stood, she kissed him, and he tasted himself on her tongue. They were now joined in every way except the most basic.

"Get on the bed," she commanded yet again then tweaked her nipples. "We've still got a long way to go."

Laney rarely remembered a time when regular sex turned her on more than being watched during the actual act. She was so revved up. No telling how many times she'd need to get off before she'd consider them prime to rest.

Not to mention, Kanoa burned hotter than hell. Already his cock seemed to be coming to life again, at one command. She loved it. *Wait, love may be too strong a word.* She shook her head.

"Is something wrong?" the big, sexy man, sprawled on the bed asked her with a look of genuine concern.

Which continued to baffle her. Somehow, their experience had this man casting aside all his previous rules when it came to dealing with people. "Nothing, except I still don't understand why I'm being treated differently."

"What do you mean?" A frown formed on his lips, matching the creases between his eyes.

She crawled onto the bed, gripping his legs and tracing them with her hands as she moved closer to his face. "You're being nice to me. You brought me here, to a room, for the night, and you're telling me you don't plan to abandon me in the morning."

"I already know everything I need to about us." He crossed his arms behind his head, propping himself up and smiling down at her.

"How do you figure?"

"Your kiss. This." He freed a hand and motioned between the two of them. "You want me for more than scenes or simply showing me off to people on camera. Coming here with me, allowing me to kiss you, shows me this is not just a one-time transaction."

His confidence unnerved her. She'd never met someone who trusted his instincts so much, and, in ways, she wanted to doubt his read of her personality or do something reckless to prove him wrong. "Really? And you think I won't call this quits tomorrow?

That I won't simply use you for a good time and then leave?"

"Because you're searching, too." He caressed her face then, gently, until he cupped her chin. "You don't say it, but I can tell from your lack of kisses, lack of intimacy. You're like me. Wanting to find someone you can be you with. I want to be yours...your someone."

Her heart clenched at his confession. This strong man, who could easily overpower her, believed—no, saw something in her he wanted. In the span of only a few hours, it seemed impossible. Yet, she'd seen many people lose out by not taking risks. "Do you really believe what you're saying?" She couldn't mistake the doubt, the fear within her words. Unavoidable, really, and she'd already been dismissed by others she'd dared to love, to give to, in the past.

"When you've been on a battlefield, you learn that moments are precious. Time is, too. You've already shown me more care, more attention, and generosity in one night than I've received from any woman I dated. Sure, those things came with white lies, but, at the heart, you were trying to help. You gave of yourself, believing I'd never be willing to accept you. Except, I do accept who you are—your likes, dislikes, and anything else you care to share with me."

Moisture pooled in her eyes, blurring his features. Strong hands gripped her arms and pulled her up until her body lay flush against his. He kissed her forehead, eyes, cheeks, neck, and then trailed upward again, stopping at her lips. The first touches were soft and gentle, but they quickly enflamed. She engaged him full-on, letting their tongues tangle in a dance they were familiar with. The urgency compounded when she felt his thick length against her belly. She wanted more than just his declarations. Words, while nice, were nothing compared to action.

"Do you have a condom?"

He reached into the drawer in the table beside the bed and pulled one out.

Taking the foil packet from his hand, she whispered, "Let me."

A rip, crinkle, and roll later, he was sheathed and she aligned him at her entrance.

"May I?"

She loved how he inquired for permission to enter instead of taking. A true sub, in all the best ways, even if he possessed less experience than others she'd been with. "Don't stop and don't come until I say you can."

He grinned, pushing in slowly. "Yes, Pretty Woman."

She gasped at the intrusion, as each inch gradually entered her and she adjusted with it. She didn't want this to be slow, though. No, for the first coupling, hard and fast were the words best used to lady take the first bite."

She opened her mouth in reception. The silky, smooth texture of the cake and the sweet strawberry topping had her eyes rolling to the back of her head. "It's delicious. Tell me, do your mother's teachings rule most of your interactions?"

"Not always." He ate a bite of dessert. "In this situation, she'd demand I make an honest woman out of you."

She smiled. "Old-fashioned to the core, huh?"

"A bit, but she always means well." He fed her another bite, and, as she chewed, crazy thoughts and images swirled in her brain. Of a wedding on a Hawaiian beach, their friends around them, and the sun setting. Thoughts about a house, and Kanoa wrestling two children, both having his tan skin and her blonde hair.

"Would it be so crazy?"

"What?" He raised an eyebrow.

Time to take the plunge. She'd most likely end up with a fresh dose of reality plus humility on her head, but.... "Marrying me. Loving me. Staying forever with me."

The fork fell from his hand and clattered against the plate.

Fuck. She'd misjudged, maybe misread everything. A kiss did not a marriage make, and she'd probably scared him off. Forget her sister taking ridiculous risks; she'd plunged off the deep end. "Never mind, forget I asked."

"We just met." He glanced at the bedside clock. "About seven hours ago. It's a little quick to jump to those decisions. Not saying I haven't had some crazy thoughts myself in the last little bit."

She waved her hand in the air in agreement. Marriage could be considered jumping the gun in a big way, time to slow it down. "How about a relationship? Is it too farfetched?"

More silence and she wanted to swallow back her words, her blunt honesty and eagerness to blurt out what she wanted. At the same time, it had needed to be said. "You're killing me with the quiet. Talk to me. Tell me what you think."

He pursed his lips and shook his head then laughed. "I think you're a dream come true, and I'm willing to take the chance if you are."

"Mission accepted."

describe the kind of sex she longed for. "Don't be gentle, pound into me."

A twist of his hips and she rolled underneath him. He used his elbows to balance himself and then acted on her commands. Her breath whooshed out of her body each time he entered, as if forcibly pulled from her. A tight, spiraling feeling, deep in her core, rose fast and ever elusive. "I'm almost there."

Kanoa's lips touched hers then his tongue. The connection, somehow, brought everything to a head, her orgasm cresting as he pulled out slowly. She clenched around him, trying to stop his exit, but he broke their kiss. "If I stay, I'll break your rule."

"Then break it." She needed to feel his release, to watch him come undone while inside her.

The response to her request involved entering her again. Nothing neat or composed, but a wild, mad pace in which he lifted her off the bed by a couple of inches, arching her body back. The head of his cock touched some special part inside her and his breathing sounded strained. She leaned up and licked his nipple. He shuddered in response then lost it. Control gone, his body jerked against hers, and she came again. Involuntarily, unable to stop the primitive reaction.

When he let her go, gently placing her back on the bed, all action ceased. They stared at each other, lost for moment. The evidence of what they'd done hit her. Experiencing release...together...something she'd rarely achieved with other partners. He'd exposed her to a huge number of firsts tonight and had stripped away the mechanisms she'd used to protect herself for so long.

"Let me get you some water." Kanoa's words broke their connection, jarring her back to reality. She had the urge to cover herself. *The exhibitionist turning shy. Lacey would laugh her ass off.*

"Sounds good." Laney pulled the top sheet loose on the bed and climbed underneath it. When he came back with not only a bottle of water but a plate of strawberry-topped cheesecake, too, her heart melted a little more. Whether she lived to regret it or not, he'd be stuck with her for a while.

"We never did get dessert, and I found this in the fridge. Courtesy of my friends, I'm sure. Didn't know if you wanted the champagne." He set the plate on the nightstand and opened her bottle of water.

She shook her head. "No, just the water."

After she took her drink, he extended a fork with a bite of cheesecake. "My mother would never forgive me if I didn't let the

Chapter One

Nothing said clean like a smooth, non-sticky bar. At least, that's what Garrett Rogers had come to define as clean. In his world, nothing ever remained perfect and orderly, except for a few certain areas he could keep tidy and limit the sphere of other people's influence. For the moment, that included this bar, until opening time.

"Howdy, partner," Lacey Malcolm's sweet, sexy Southern drawl rang out through the empty room, echoing off the walls. His pants got tighter.

"Afternoon to you, too. I had no clue you were here." A little white lie—he always kept track of anyone in the building. The other half of his business required it. His doorman, Ron, who slept on the second floor, was out for the afternoon, taking care of personal business. Leaving him alone with her, and damn if she didn't pull those painted, luscious red lips into a saucy grin.

"The dungeon needed straightening, especially if I'm going to entertain company tonight. Bless Laney's heart, but she and Kanoa aren't the best at tidying up."

"You mean they aren't OCD like a certain Domme standing in front of me?"

She didn't respond to his question but slid up on a barstool and propped her elbows on the pine bar top, her pale, creamy skin perfection. Damn, he needed to rein in his wayward thoughts.

"Who are you entertaining tonight?" He clenched his jaw. Why did he have to ask the one question bound to give him anxiety?

"My date with Madame Eve's 1Night Stand service. I've got positive vibes." She tugged on the bottom of her pastel-blue, Tweety Bird-dotted scrub top before brushing her blonde ponytail off her shoulder. "The second time is the charm."

Unbelievable. He slapped his hands against the bar. The glasses stored on a shelf underneath rattled. "Are you kidding me? You dodged a bullet the first round. Why take a risk like that?"

She frowned. "I'm going to ignore the fact you just insulted my sister's man and then I'll remind you this is my one chance."

"One chance?"

"To find someone who wants me for me. Let's face it, Garrett. Around here, everyone knows who I am. Finding someone willing to see past my need for perfection, my serious nature, my quirks.... I'm aware of my long list of flaws. I need to get a guy who can see the real me underneath."

He shook his head and threw the wet towel on the floor. This woman had been driving him crazy ever since Victoria's wedding a few months ago. That night he'd almost kissed Lacey — almost being the most annoying word of the century. "Honey, I think you're putting a little too much pressure on this stranger you're meeting. If anything, this would be the first date of many. A chance for you to start building something."

"It's called 1Night Stand." Lacey laughed. "And I'm going to get my full one night out of it. I'm paying enough. I also believe successful relationships require not just physical compatibility but mental as well. Whoever this guy is, he's already aware of my proclivities and will want to experience them."

For an intelligent dental hygienist and attentive Domme, she sometimes demonstrated a severe lack in common sense and observation skills. Plus, she tended to keep her sex life very private, something he'd been aware of for years but never experienced firsthand. Nor had he wanted to — until their dance at the wedding. "So, what's his name?"

"Logan. I've been told three things about him. He owns a home, believes honesty and communication skills are the most attractive things about a female, and enjoys new experiences."

"Pretty vague if you ask me." He snorted. The woman had set herself up to be taken advantage of. Duty bound, and for selfish reasons, he'd already ensured such a thing wouldn't happen. "Enjoys new experiences could detail wanting to kidnap beautiful women or lick their toes."

She winked at him. "I've always been interested in role-play but never found the right sub."

No stopping this one from a potential train wreck. She'd been headed in the same direction since college. Once she made up her mind, nothing could prevent her from following the path toward her goal. Even her twin had failed to derail the machinations of this bombshell's grand schemes, multiple times over. Funny how none of those ideas ever involved a relationship until now. "Remind me again who turned you on to this whole thing."

"Victoria. 1Night Stand and the infamous Madame Eve are the reason she reconciled with Royce. A true love story. So I figure, why not? Life's not worth living unless you take risks."

"I'd say that's something we can both agree on." Garrett held his hand out to her, a last-ditch effort for connection and maybe a chance to change her mind. She slapped her palm against his, and he resisted the urge to press a kiss to the back of her soft hand. "Good luck tonight. I know I can't change your mind, but there are men who want you for you. I'm one of them."

The smile drained from her face, replaced with wide-eyed shock and followed by fear. Hell, she even bit her lower lip. Then she pulled away, hand and gaze, dismissing him. He almost regretted being so blunt, but he wanted her to have the knowledge, the truth, about what he wanted before tonight. Before things went too far down another road.

Taking a deep breath, she stood from the barstool then turned to face him. "I appreciate your honesty, but we're best friends and I don't want to ruin our bond."

"I understand." He'd show her.

"Night, Garrett. I'll see you later."

Yes, she would.

***

Lacey had blown through the glass of Cabernet the bartender served her in less than ten minutes. Instead of asking for a refill, she decided to pace herself. After all, she'd been given the moniker "Ice Queen" for being a tough Domme and career woman. Waiting for another glass of wine demonstrated her formidable restraint. She didn't do nervous, timid, or half a dozen other emotions associated with her gender either, which would explain why she classified the gut-wrenching feeling moving its way through her insides as indigestion. Maybe the wine caused her discomfort, hence no more libations until she got some food in her.

Anyone who knew the intimate side of her could guess why she'd picked Levi's, a gastropub in downtown Rogers, with little-to-no problem. It laid the framework for running into someone she knew, setting herself up for an easy out. If Victoria had been here, she'd have called Lacey out as a fake. She never took true risks, incapable of embracing the definition of spontaneity. As soon as someone mentioned the idea of something—anything—she planned the next steps, which clicked into place like whitening trays on teeth. According to her sister, she possessed a bad habit, one she'd never rid herself of. The mere idea of going on a date with someone unfamiliar fell into the spontaneous-as-she-got column. Then the question played again in her mind. Why are you doing this?

Garrett, jerk and endearing friend, had asked her the same thing half a dozen times. Almost every time they talked. She wanted to be surprised, to escape herself and her own machinations. To push through her fears of intimacy, of being rejected. Funny how even when she tried to be off guard, spur of the moment, she still planned contingencies for all possible ways this evening could go down—because the "bad habit" of protecting herself came as natural as brushing her teeth. Sure Garrett believed her actions to be unsafe and putting herself in danger. He obviously didn't have enough faith in her OCD ways when it came to ensuring her heart and body stayed safe.

Thinking of her friend reminded her of all the reasons she'd been pissed at him, including the ones from today. He'd been acting strange ever since they filled in as each other's dates to Victoria's wedding, which equaled the worst and best mistake she'd made in a while. Worst, because their multiple dances and side-by-side dinner seating tore away the curtain covering their friendship. For the first time, she regarded him with "attraction" eyes, not with the simple "friendship" eyes she'd always viewed him with. Turned out her college friend could be attentive, kind, and really good at treating her like the only woman in the room. He'd never done such a thing before. Of course, top everything off with a hefty helping of drop-dead gorgeous and he presented a tempting package.

And the almost kiss.... An image of his lips filled her mind...big, smooth, pink, and inches from her own during the last dance of the night. If she'd had the courage to close the gap, it would've happened.

She shook her head. No, better it hadn't. We both enjoy dominance, and there are too many obstacles in the river between us. Instead, the evening left her with longing for the chance to have a similar relationship, a real one, with someone. But dating and Lacey did not mix well. Here's to hoping tonight will play out better.

She glanced toward the front door, and her gaze fell on a single red rose held within a strong, tanned hand. Madame Eve's text mentioned her date would be holding a rose. She traced from the crimson flower to his black slacks then up to his button-down red shirt, black tie, and then, at last, his face.

Shit. A nightmare come true. Garret, sexy smile and all, owned the hot body clutching her rose. Except, the rust-colored beard he wore—it'd been shaved off. He approached her, slow, confident, and irritating. She wanted to yell, maybe do him bodily harm. Instead, she took a deep breath. The best way to keep control of a situation involved staying on top of her emotions.

"Good evening." She offered up the greeting first, doing her damnedest to put a smile on her face.

Garrett extended the rose to her. "Hi. I brought this for you."

She took the flower synonymous with love, passion, and great respect. Did he mean those things when he decided to present one to her? "Thank you. Now, what the hell are you doing here?"

"I have a date, with you."

"You know what I mean. I want some explanations." The volume of her voice went up a few decibels, unintentional and uncontrollable. Several couples occupying barstools on either side of them cast wayward glances or frowned.

"How about you get up and go with me to our table? I might consider answering your questions if you say please. Or I can announce this for everyone to hear. Your choice."

"Fine. But if it doesn't measure up, I'm out of here." She'd also be asking for a refund or another date. This was the second time things failed to work in her favor, and her mind raced as she followed the hostess to their little two-seat alcove behind a paper partition. "This isn't part of the restaurant. Why are we here?"

"Does it matter? This is our table. You want answers." Nodding at the hostess, Garrett waited until she left them then pulled out a chair and gestured for Lacey to sit down. Glass lamps hung low over the thick, stain-glossed square walnut tables, illuminating a pair of glasses and a decorative wine bottle filled with water. Music from an Americana band filtered from the other side of the room, but, thanks to the partition, they wouldn't need to yell to hear each other.

Damn him. She acquiesced this time, and he slid her chair under the table with ease. If he thought she'd follow his commands with ease from here on out, he would get a rude awakening. "Now, please explain to me why you're here and not Logan."

"I am Logan...Garrett Rogers. On my application, I listed my legal name, but everyone has always called me by my middle one, so I wouldn't get confused with my father. Thought I told you my given name when we met?" He picked up his menu then, cutting off any visual contact.

"Must have slipped your mind." He'd tricked her, used her, and for what fucking purpose? "Like telling me you planned on manipulating me like some sub with a fetish."

The menu came down about a half an inch, exposing those stormy-gray eyes of his. "If I'd told you about tonight, about me being your date, would you have shown up?"

She hesitated, reaching up to touch the bun at the back of her head, making sure the coiled hair held tight. The urge to lie and say yes sat on the tip of her tongue. Yet, she abhorred lying...at least most of the time. This might be one of the times she'd be willing to do it.

"Don't you think about telling me a fib, Lace."

Faking surprise, she batted her lashes and went for demure. "Why, I'd never."

"The hair touching says otherwise. Remember, I've seen you lie before. Do it now, and I'll make you pay for it later." He thought mighty high of himself, threatening her like a random sub. So, he earned the truth.

"Nope, I'd have canceled right away because this is silly and foolishness. We're incompatible." She lifted a glass of ice water to her lips, hoping a sip would cool her heated skin. The way he talked sometimes, the way he knew her made the air seem stuffy.

"I don't think wanting you is any one of those things."

She coughed as a splash of water went down the wrong tube. No way had she heard him right. "What did you say?"

"I. Want. You."

Chapter Two

From the moment he'd seen her, she'd stolen his sanity from him, piece by piece. Every word, every look, every damn infuriating expression threatened his patience and resolve to make her submit, to succumb. He longed for one shot at her submission, something she'd never given anyone, even him. Yet, she'd failed to yield control, except for the moment where she sat in the chair. Such a thing gave him hope. Not a ton of it, but enough to continue. Now, he'd uttered the one sentence he'd kept to himself for over two months, and she wanted it clarified.

He could do that. "I. Want. You."

She set the glass back on the table. "Why?"

Well played. "Because I do. That should suffice. What sounds good to you?" He didn't want to examine all the reasons out loud. All five of them had played around in his head multiple times over the last eight weeks. They kept him from engaging in D/s sessions, had him turning away clients he'd worked with for years, and left him with continuous fantasies he wanted to make realities.

"No. You don't get to change the subject. I want an answer." She tapped her fingers on the table. A relentless, delicious woman bundled up in a cerulean-blue dress with black stiletto-heeled, strapped boots. She'd swept up her platinum-blonde hair, wrapping it into a tight bun with wisps falling in a random pattern, framing her face. The slender, elegant slope of her neck adorned by pearls. She channeled elegance. Would those pearls serve well as a gag?

Then and there he decided to give her answers, but only if he got cooperation. "How about this. I'll give you my reasons, but you have to order a drink, dinner, dessert, and answer two of my questions."

"You're asking a lot."

"I'm asking for five things. One thing for each of my reasons for wanting you." Such a sentence got a shiver out of her, starting at her collarbone and working its way through her shoulders then down her body. He missed seeing it shimmy out of her legs but figured

137

the best offense would be to make her believe he didn't see how she'd been affected. He waited, glancing between the menu he'd refused to set down this entire time and her face.

A horrible poker player, her internal debate danced its way through a series of different expressions. Until, a moment later, she smiled and slid the menu off the table. "All right. I'll do it."

He kept his sigh of relief internal. His poker face rivaled those of even seasoned players. Evidenced by his successful contract negotiations for his bar and the ranch he owned. "I hear the cheeseburger is amazing."

"Sounds delicious. I'll take the same and a Jameson neat." She returned the menu to the table, and the damn minx never even looked at it. "Now, tell me the first two reasons."

"I'm surprised you've become such an impressive, sought-after Domme with what little patience you exhibit."

"You call it impatience. I call it no more time to waste on fucking around." The words came out with a low growl, and his pants tightened. She had no clue how much she hit all the right buttons, ones he'd kept concealed until this night.

"Fine. The first reason is Victoria's wedding."

The waiter arrived before he could go on. Perfect timing. He provided a small basket of rolls, took their order, and then left. Efficient little bastard, he deserved a good tip. But damn it if Garrett didn't want a few more minutes of hemming and hawing over dinner choices before diving into what he didn't want to discuss.

"Continue." Another demand uttered from perfect red lips. Lips he'd almost kissed.

Fine, to hell with it. "We were wonderful together. I don't know about you, but I've never had so much fun at a wedding. Even dancing and mingling proved less of a chore with you there. I want a chance for more of the same." Without the menu, he'd exposed himself, words and visage, for her perusal and censor. He glanced at the ceiling for a few seconds, summoning courage and the same attitude he used all the time in the dungeon. "You felt it, too."

Lacey smiled, a genuine, ear-to-ear smile. "This happened to be the first wedding we ever went to together. How can you know the atmosphere of the moment didn't play a part in those emotions?"

"So, you admit to the intimacies, then? We are marvelous."

"A natural reaction to the evening. A simple explanation." She shook her head. "I'd have done the same with anyone."

Fine, she wanted to play hardball. "Reason number two, we're both looking for someone. A special someone to start a relationship with. Why not start with a person who's on the same wavelength already? After the wedding, I realized I'd reached the time to settle down, but I need to be with someone compatible."

"We're not compatible."

He'd run through their differences a million times in his head. It didn't rid him of the memories of her scent, her eyes, and the way her body fit against his.

"This is lust you're experiencing, Garrett. Nothing more and it's natural. I'll even admit to a few fleeting moments after we spent the evening, at a wedding no less. The ultimate touchy-feely-emotional baggage-fest. I don't—"

"Treat other people like simpletons, including those fools sitting in your dentist chair day in and day out with mouths like garbage disposals, but give me a little more respect than those idiots."

Her jaw hung open, still locked mid-sentence. Then she hunched her eyebrows and frowned. "I'll give you respect when you learn to stop interrupting people like a toddler. See what I'm talking about? Right here, incompatible. And up until this whole 'I want you' crap started, we never had a problem."

"We've always had problems." They'd been butting heads since he'd trained her, their mouths always at odds. Not in intimacy, as he'd like it, but with verbal sparring. "You try to control everything and you keep arguing when I won't budge. It happens all the time."

"Because you're stubborn."

The waiter brought the drinks then, and they both shut up. Garrett ran a hand through this short hair, tugging on the ends. He took a sip of his bourbon, trying to decide the next route to take. Lacey refused to give an inch, something to admire on one hand and despise on the other. "All I'm asking for is one night."

"One night?" She ran her index finger along the rim of her glass, slow and deliberate. "What would this consist of?"

Thank God. Such a question meant she was considering it. "You submitting to me."

139

She laughed. "That's the funniest thing I've heard you say. Ever."

"I'm serious."

Her head cocked to the side, and her brows furrowed. "Need I remind you the Dom who trained me tried to get me to go through submission once and I proved I didn't need to?"

"As said trainer, I still believe you need to go through submission one time."

Verbal silence ruled the table, with both of them taking sips of their whiskey. She tapped her foot, drummed fingers, glanced around the room, stared at him. He refused to take his eyes off her in the interim. Wanting her to experience the discomfort, the stress, coupled with the decision.

Just as the waiter approached the table with their dinner, she announced, "Fine, but if I submit, you'll have to, too."

She loved the look on his face, the wide-eyed shock at the mere idea of submitting. "See? You like the idea as much as I do."

Lacey leaned back, and the waiter set her plate in front of her, a couple of frites spilling off the side onto the table. She didn't hesitate to cut into the burger, focusing on the food instead of Garrett. While she sliced through the bun, beef, and cheese, she imagined him refusing her offer. Of course, she'd accept his decision and allow their friendship to get back on track. He'd be chastised properly and no more crazy ideas of trying to start a relationship between them any deeper than the bond they already shared. He didn't understand what losing him would do to her; going deeper and breaking boundaries already established would ensure the loss. She gave a short nod, pointed at her plate then took the bite.

The juicy beef tasted salty and sweet thanks to the bacon on top. Coupled with the thick slice of cheddar cheese, the myriad of flavors overwhelmed the senses.

"Fine, I agree," Garrett announced, interrupting her food bliss.

Her fork clattered against the porcelain plate. She strived to stay in control, to breathe in an easy manner, but a tight knot took up residence in her chest. She dismissed it as a bite of food gone down wrong—anything else meant disaster. Lacey had always believed she was good at recognizing emotions in others, whereas she tended to ignore her own at all costs. "You don't mean that."

"I'm afraid I do. If it's the one way you'll give me a chance, then so be it." He took a bite of his burger. It'd be a lie to say they didn't have things in common, a taste for burgers being one. In fact, they'd always had similar tastes in movies, music, and even hobbies.

She shook her head. No, it wouldn't work, and now he'd accepted. She'd been so focused on shutting him down, angling for a way to get him to refuse, but she'd failed to consider he'd accept her challenge. "You desire this?"

"I'd think it obvious. I spelled it out, gave you two reasons why, and you still doubt me. I think the real question here is why you don't believe me."

Good question. Maybe it had to do with the fact he'd never shown interest in her before, at least until the wedding. He'd always been the dependable friend, her trainer and mentor in D/s, and, together, they'd swapped stories, drunk, hung out from time to time. If she agreed to pursue a relationship, losing him would turn from fiction to reality, guaranteed. She didn't want to give up someone from her personal group for the sake of possibilities. The best way to explore a relationship was with a person she wouldn't care to lose. Someone unaware of all her horrible habits and the way they'd take over all the time.

Outside of those facts, she fell far from a sub. He never categorized himself as a submissive either. How the hell would the bedroom work? Vanilla sex went out the window for her when Garrett introduced her to his kinky world. She'd had the inkling before then but no way to channel it. Giving someone else control— the option didn't exist. As her musing went on, gooseflesh broke out on her skin, her hands trembling against the table as his eyes watched her like a hawk. "I believe you. It's just.... The bedroom piece. It'd never work."

"So, you're saying you'd be willing to try."

Holy hell, when he looked like that—smile and eyes bright with joy—she couldn't imagine saying no, extinguishing his light. "A date is one thing...."

"Yes, it is, and, as far as submission, I'm asking for a night. Let me show you how it can be. This is just one night."

"Just a scene? No sex."

He chuckled, a low, seductive rumble that vibrated through the table and into her body. "When I said I wanted you, I meant all of you. Sex included, and we let the scene move us. Instinct will be our guide."

It amazed her at how easy he made it sound. Like a simple thing, even when the idea of kneeling, being restrained or deprived caused a widespread riot in her very being. The sole person she could think of giving such a deep level of trust would be her sister. Instead, Garrett had asked her to give him the honor. She'd seen him with other subs. Conscientious, purposeful, and knowledgeable the best words to describe his dominance. Their running joke during her training had been she wanted to be like him when she grew up. Yet, commonality between them ended with age. Her kink, her sadism ran toward another vein. She liked pain, inflicting it, more than anything. How could she inflict pain by being restrained, and how could she get off? Holy shit!

As she looked at Garrett, she pored over the possibilities instead of shooting down the idea, and, by the bastard's smirk, he knew it, too.

"Once we cross this bridge, there won't be any chance of going back." No chance of preserving their friendship. Did she want to give him up for sex?

Another bite of food, followed by a sip of his Jameson, and then he winked at her. "I'm planning on going forward. I'm going to blow the damn thing up and construct something more lasting."

Ha. He'd lost his damn mind. "What's more lasting than a bridge?"

"A future." His expression somber, his eyes bored into hers as if trying to communicate some unspoken message. The look scared her, more than it should. Why in the world she hadn't already run out the door, vowing to escape somewhere far away, told her maybe she'd developed a bit of a daredevil streak. And you want this.

Deep down, her desires twisted like a tangled coil of rope—a straight-up mess. She didn't want to open that can of worms. To do so meant riding down a slippery slope.

"Are you okay?" Garrett's deep bass flowed over her like maple syrup poured on waffles. Made her feel soggy, spongy enough to fall in line. She'd fallen prey to his game, and Lacey Malcolm needed help.

"I'm fine."

"You were staring off into space, brows hunched, and looking frustrated. Don't start lying to me now."

She bit her lower lip for a moment then grabbed her whiskey and downed the rest. "To be honest, you've got me a little freaked out."

"How so?"

"This whole proposal, and I'm anxious, nervous...scared."

Reaching across the table, he encircled her pale-peach wrist with his bronzed fingers. The man spent too much time in the sun. "You know I'd never do anything to hurt you."

"I've always trusted you." Too a point. As she did with everyone, best friends, family, or co-workers.... The list ran a mile long. When you kept people at arm's length, they couldn't be turned off or disturbed by your personality.

"Then do so now. Believe I'll provide you with comfort and fun. For now, let's forget about all this and enjoy the food."

Smiling, Lacey gave his hand a gentle squeeze. He'd always been as stubborn as she, and, with the bargain struck, she wouldn't back out. But she'd never give up everything, nor would she trust him with their future. "All right. I can do that."

Chapter Three

Garrett enjoyed the hell out of dinner from the moment she capitulated. He didn't take pleasure in scaring her, though. After he'd provided reassurance, the tension radiating around them melted away. Talk, in between bites, moved toward their jobs from her dental patients to his time spent on the ranch. The fact she asked questions about his animals, his future plans for developing the land, and that she cared reminded him of why he wanted this so much. This—stimulating conversation, someone who gave a damn.

"When did you sign up for the service?" Her question threw him for a loop.

He'd always been honest with Lacey, with the exception of this date, and he wouldn't stop now. "After your first foray turned out a bust. I knew what I wanted, and I filled my application out with exactly that."

"Wait, you said on your app you wanted me?"

He couldn't tell if she thought this admission sweet or stalker-ish. He'd be the first to admit his actions may have been a little strange. "I get it. It's a little crazy and weird for me to put that, but I did. I told the whole story from before, the wedding, and now."

"You're right, it's insane, and I'm floored. I can't decide whether to be mad or over the moon."

He grinned. "I like over the moon myself." Silence ruled, and she broke eye contact, busying herself with her napkin. Lacey didn't act this way on a regular basis. No, she mastered the scene as the outspoken one, the daredevil, and ever the Dominant in every way. Her actions irked him. "Care for dessert?"

"Can't say I'm in the mood for anything sweet. You?" Hooded eyes accompanied those words.

"Are you playing me?"

"Whatever are you talking about?" She batted her lashes.

Damn. "Too good to be true. And of course you want to pretend you're someone else. Quit playing innocent, sweet miss. I don't want a fake you. Things were fine until a few minutes ago," he growled.

She laughed, the loud, melodic sound echoing around the walls. "You should have seen your face. Just testing you. And you didn't fall for it."

"Testing me? Why?" If she pulled this kind of crap with any man wanting a date, he'd be infuriated. She should know him better by now.

"You said it yourself…. Your current behavior isn't normal at the moment. Testing your sincerity seemed like the right move. Plus, I'm still not 100 percent sure about going forward."

He signaled to the waiter for the check, still upset. Her actions spoke of mistrust and secrets whether she'd admit it or not. Now, she had him doubting his belief in this whole thing. What if he'd read her wrong all these years? Or maybe she practiced a bit of sadism outside of the dungeon? Pulling out his wallet, he slapped down the cash to cover the bill and the tip. Then he stood.

Lacey watched him, her mouth opening and closing several times. Good. At least she chose to pay attention to his mood. To be aware he didn't appreciate her lack of faith in him. "I'm sorry. Don't leave yet."

"Who said I was leaving?"

She huffed. "You jackass."

"Oh, I'm many things, but since I just paid for dinner, you could be nicer." He slipped around to her side of the table, putting himself in the line of fire from her perfume, a maddening, floral scent she wore. The smell had tied into arousal for him ever since they'd plastered themselves together on the dance floor at the wedding. He leaned in and whispered in her ear. "I'm going to walk out the door. If you're still prepared for one night, then you come with me. If you don't follow, I leave and we chalk this up to a nice date. But you're right."

She shivered as he watched, goose bumps pebbling on her neck, along with the small hairs standing on end. He wanted to touch, to tease the area. "Right about what?"

"Whatever happens, tonight changes everything." He headed toward the front entrance, dodging past a couple walking in the door. The lounge traffic had picked up, and a few people even milled outside on the sidewalk. The spring air, a little warmer than typical for March, wrapped around him. He'd lucked out with a parking spot just off to the left side of the restaurant. So she had no time to decide whether or not this would happen. Five steps outside the restaurant door, he heard the clack of heels on the concrete.

"Garrett, wait!" Her words came like a message from above. Crystal clear, and with a hint of determination. Maybe he was reading too much into it, but he wanted to believe she'd chased him because, otherwise, this would be the last super-personal interaction they had. She caught up to him and gripped his shoulder tight. "I'm coming with you."

He stopped and faced her, all of the five foot and five inches, flushed pink, blue-dress-wearing beauty. "Then you agree to the terms. We start now, the scene begins. You submit. No waiting, no more games."

"But after I'm done, then you'll submit to me."

Garrett nodded. "Agreed. As long as you don't hold back."

"I won't."

He grinned at his success. Next, he'd test the freedom. "Then, walk in front of me, no words, and go to the passenger side door of my truck." With where he'd parked, that side of the truck would be blocked from the front entrance of the restaurant and street.

She did as instructed, executing a slow, seductive strut, rounding the side of the building, and stopping in front of the passenger side door to his F-150 double-extended cab, black pickup. He'd be lying by trying to deny his erection or the fierce desire to have her this second. Unlike his Dominant counterparts, he didn't need a scene to do the deed. No, he could have tantalizing sex without any provocation. The irony was he'd never known Lacey to be the same way. She always hid within a scene to get her jollies off.

He refused to let her hide. Right. Now. "Turn and put your arms against the truck, palms flat."

"But—"

"I said no talking."

She went through the motions, her expression showing frustration.

"Now, spread your legs by two inches."

The great thing about both of them being Dominants was she knew the measurements and all the directions as well as an understanding of the instinct to follow—she'd never confess to such a thing, though. Once her legs were the proper distance, he leaned in, trailing the tip of his tongue along the shell of her ear, as his wandering fingers moved up the inside of her bare thigh and underneath the hemline of her dress. Instead of encountering panties or a thong, he found her bare. Such a brave statement deserved a reward, so he nipped her ear. "You sat there, exposed like this, and never told me."

"It's a surprise, or at least I planned it to be." Her words came out in short breaths, and, judging from the moisture he found when he reached the apex of her thighs, she found this encounter as arousing as he did.

"Well, consider this my surprise." He inserted two digits into her opening, pounding them into her without preamble. Then followed up by flicking her clit with his thumb. She moaned, her purse making a small crinkling noise as she clutched it tight and put more pressure on the truck door. He gave her the side of his other palm to bite on. "You need to keep it down or you'll give us away."

Her teeth sank into his flesh hard, and he growled, continuing his onslaught to her vagina. Her leg muscles tightened, and her feet arched. She tensed against him, and then her orgasm crested. She shook, refusing to let go of her grip on his flesh, in both her mouth and below. He pulled out and brought his hand to his mouth, licking her cum from his fingers. She angled her head, watching him, and then relaxed her jaw enough for him to pull his hand out.

"Thank you." He flexed his fingers, trying to shake away the imprint of her teeth and the residual pain pulsating through his muscles as he reached into his suit coat for his keys and unlocked the truck. "Hop in."

She tugged at her hemline, opened the door, and gave her best attempt to get into the truck without flashing him a perfect view of her labia. No luck there, but he played the gentleman and shut the door behind her. When he hopped up next to her, she looked straight out the windshield, arms crossed, and her expression blank.

"Talk to me. Tell me how you feel." Key in ignition, the whole vehicle rumbled as the engine roared to life.

"I just came in a restaurant parking lot where we could have been caught. I'm not sure how I feel."

He'd let it go for a few minutes and focused on backing out of the lot and heading toward his home. The LGR ranch sat in the township of Centerton, west of the major development in Bentonville and Rogers, where wilderness still held an edge, and it wouldn't be much to find a big cat, a small deer herd, or even a bear wandering the property. A little over sixty acres his father and mother had gifted him before they retired to sunny Florida. A successful rancher, his father had sold Angus, organic beef, and had cornered the market at the right time, right place. No problems existed as long as Garrett maintained everything.

As they passed the last stoplight on the small stretch of country highway, he pressed the accelerator and asked again, "Did you find the experience horrible? Embarrassing?"

"Unexpected is the word I'd use. Along with the phrase not-my-style." She twirled the ends of the ponytail she'd released from its bun. The dashboard lights lit her face with a soft glow.

"You were amazing, if my opinion helps at all. For someone not fond of outdoor intimacy, you could've fooled me." He grinned. "Why unexpected?"

"You have a lot of questions." Annoyance filled her voice.

"I told you, we're burning the old bridge and building a new one. This includes more talking and more details. Tell me."

She sighed. "I don't get off without pain…and I did. It's a new experience."

Her confession made him proud and determined to repeat the act. "The hope is tonight will be filled with more of those."

"Yes, but, if you recall, sometimes opening up doorways to things outside of one's comfort zone may not always bring the best results."

He hit his high beams as the last of the lights from the town faded, illuminating the entire road. She'd started talking riddles. "What do you mean?"

"I mean, maybe I'm not as awesome as you think I am."

"You've been pretty damn wonderful since the day I met you. I'm just sorry it took so long for me to realize it. So whatever you think I'll find horrible, remember I want you as is, always."

"Be careful what you wish for." She sounded doubtful.

The word wish made him think of the noise she'd made in the parking lot. Would she sound the same when he brought her to orgasm with his cock? Therein lay the problem. He'd been hard since their little escapade, and in desperate need of release.

He turned off onto a side road, a back way to his property. With one hand, he undid his belt buckle then released the button and lowered the zipper on his slacks, releasing his erection from confinement, all without taking his gaze from the road. Sure, he'd slowed to ten miles an hour—no sense in hurrying. No rush at all.

"What are you doing?" Curiosity replaced the earlier doubt, and she leaned forward in her seat.

"Relieving a little pressure." He stroked his thick length. "Back in the parking lot, you weren't the only one affected."

He stroked without shame, ever aware of the increasing tension in the cab, swirling tight around them—similar to how she'd feel sheathing him with either her mouth or her sweet vag. He'd always possessed a bit of an exhibitionist streak, but never displayed it nor gave into it. Seemed tonight would be a night filled with a lot of firsts. For Lacey and for him.

She almost swallowed her tongue when he wrapped his hand around his cock. Sure, in the parking lot she'd gotten an impression of his package through his pants against her leg, but she'd never had the pleasure to view it firsthand. There were stories, of course. She and her sister were privy to them time and again from several different subs who enjoyed bragging by waggling eyebrows or using a show of hands. Until tonight, she'd never given it thought, but now, as she watched Garrett continue to stroke in a methodical, slow-paced fashion, every single visual description about his erection and its capabilities rushed back full force.

She licked her lips, and he glanced at her then swerved the wheel and slammed the brakes, bringing them to a stop in the middle of the road.

"Well, at least we know the brakes work." She made the comment as an attempt at lightening the very sensual mood swamping her being. Erotic tension hung in the air of the cab, thanks to him and his large erection.

"Yes, and I'm thankful these work, too." He switched the headlights off, the low glow from the dash becoming the sole source of light for miles.

She fidgeted in her seat for a moment, trying to get her libido under control. With no success. "We're stopped in the middle of the road. Someone could crash into us."

"No one travels out here this late at night except me and the wildlife." He unlatched his seat belt and crooked a finger at her. "Come here."

His low voice and two-word command, along with his wolfish stare, did something to her insides. He looked determined, and horny as hell. A look she inspired, no doubt. He may have been calling the shots, but at the heart of the situation, she remained in control.

Garrett tended to rule his sessions beyond closed doors. Tonight, he'd gotten her off with some rough finger banging and pretty words. She had no clue what he planned, but she'd agreed to this and, Lord help her, some depraved part of her enjoyed seeing him lose control when he thought himself in possession of it.

She pressed the button on her seat-belt latch, the polyester belt loosened around her, and she shrugged out of it. Slipping her heels off her feet, the strappy shoes clunked against the floorboard, each thump echoing in the background. Then she crawled across the bench seat, thankful he preferred automatics and she didn't have to traverse a stick shift.

His breath grew harsh as her breasts brushed against his upper arm.

"Sir?"

He groaned at the honorific, resting his forehead against hers. "I desire you. Now."

So primitive and caveman-like. Instead of being repulsed, the words called to her, awoke something torturous in her Dominant demeanor, and she found herself unable to resist, giving into it— without shame. "How? Tell me how you desire me."

He angled to the side, breaking their connection, and a small metal creak filled the cab as the driver's seat slid back a few inches. "Ride me."

Lacey straddled him, sliding her dress up, exposing her bare ass. He grabbed each cheek, squeezing and kneading, using his grip to guide her onto him, and, as he slid home, she gasped. Holy hell, this position—sitting upright—didn't fall within her preferred arrangements. The angle perfect, the width of him filling, she wanted to hold this moment. Freeze it to replay later. Then he moved, releasing his hold on her bottom, adjusting to place a hand on each of her hips, and waited.

"Open your eyes."

She did and found herself staring into twin gray, swirling storms. Dark near the center and light around the edges, his eyes focused on her with severe intensity. Grabbing his shoulders, she anchored her balance then lifted up. The separation brought a gasp from both of their lips, as if in pain because they were no longer joined. Plunging down again provided relief, and so the dance continued. He never touched her beyond her hips and allowed her to call the shots on pace. This whole interaction seemed unnatural, in fact...it was more vanilla than anything else, and that she couldn't allow.

The bliss of the joining faded, and, while she rode toward oblivion, she decided to inject a bit of their game play into the moment. So, she smacked his face. Not once, but twice. Loving the sting of her flesh hitting his. He growled at her and broke the momentum she'd provided. The returning strikes to her ass cheeks were double what she'd given him, and she yelled with each one. Then he pounded into her. No remorse, no reprieve, until she came screaming his name.

A few more jerks and his body stiffened as his release stormed free. He pulled her off him and jetted his cum between their bodies, smearing them both with evidence of his pleasure and giving her a reason to burn this dress. But the burning party would wait until tomorrow. For now, she slid back into her seat and secured her seat belt once more.

She'd crossed a line, topped from bottom, and done so blatantly. Yet, he'd engaged in intercourse without setting the rules. How the hell did she let herself get so wrapped up she rode him bareback?

The lack of words, and altogether noise inside the cab, set the mood—pissed. The man's temper almost never flared to the surface, but her friend was ten times more dangerous when silent. He zipped up and pounded both palms flat against the dash. When the truck started moving again, she chose to remain silent and ponder his actions as well as her own.

Within moments, she concluded her body had turned traitor, and she'd do well not to trust its reactions in the future.

Chapter Four

Garrett pulled into his driveway, still not ready to talk. He'd disregarded her safety for a fuck—his number-one rule thrown away because of a look in a woman's eyes. Trying to convince himself it happened because he'd been hands-off in a scene and with his body for more than a month would be the ultimate lie. Truth be told, he'd become obsessed with the idea of sex, domination, and submission with Lacey Malcolm.

He yanked his keys out of the ignition, hopped out of the cab, and slammed the truck door. Maybe she'd be the smarter of the two of them and stay inside the truck. Hell, after he downed some ice water to cool his body down, maybe he'd give her the keys and tell her to head into town. In the morning, his bouncer could take him to pick up the pickup. Ha.

The joke calmed him long enough to get the key in the lock and unlatch the dead bolt. Then his mistakes came rushing back. They'd never discussed limits, precautions, and all the other things. The rules of the Playroom meant regular testing—any good dungeon required it. He had at least an inch-thick file on every member, detailing experiences, limits, kinks, and all manner of stuff. Still, he felt dirty in a way for treating her different than the others—though, to him, she was different.

He threw his keys on the little table inside the door, slipped off his shoes, and headed for the kitchen and the ice-cold beverage waiting for him.

"You want me to lock the front door?" Her voice echoed in the little foyer, permeating his being and awaking his cock. Again.

He took a deep breath, and, in those few seconds, decided to follow this through to the end—regardless of the consequences. If she refused to back down, then neither would he. "Sure. I'm getting a bottle of water. Want anything?"

"Water sounds good." She followed him, the click-clack of her heels tapping on the hardwood.

Reaching into the stainless steel monstrosity of a refrigerator, he pulled out twin two liter bottles filled with water and handed her one.

"Still drinking out of these big things?" She laughed and grabbed the red bottle, spinning the cap off the top and onto the counter.

In their world, hydration was important for any type of playtime. Water promoted healing and longevity. "I save them for after a workout. Drink up."

The first blast of cold hit his mouth and offered the oasis he wanted, a nice cooling sensation as he gulped the liquid. When he opened his eyes, the relief he'd sought shriveled and died against the vision of Lacey swallowing small sips of water and letting the rest leak down her chin, soaking her dress and plastering it to her body. Her nipples pebbled against the fabric, the stains from his release lightened in color, and droplets dripped on the floor. Damn.

She pulled the bottle from her lips and set it on the counter, empty. "That did the trick." Then she glanced down, a devious grin on her face. "Oops, I guess you'll have to punish me."

He bit his lower lip, hard. Almost drawing blood. The urge to strip her of the dress and leave marks all over her body with her wet clothing threatened to become reality. He opened his mouth to speak the commands, but, instead, said, "Lacey, why are you still going along with this?"

Some things she knew. Garrett liked her body, worshipped it, in fact—evidenced by his lack of restraint so far. Her friend also enjoyed being teased. They'd been doing it in a nonsexual manner for years, so she'd taken pleasure in discovering how naturally it came to do the same thing now. All with the knowledge and hope the demanding creature from the truck, the one who couldn't wait to have her, would make an appearance.

Call her downright twisted—in fact, her sister did—but.... "You said in the truck you desired me. I have to admit I'd like to see how far that desire goes."

"But.... No, I didn't talk to you first. We didn't discuss anything about our preferences." He threw the half-empty two liter in the kitchen sink. Water splashed as it hit. "Damn it. I put your safety at risk with that stunt in the truck. I almost didn't pull out in time."

She reached for him, and, when her fingertips touched his arm, he came toward her in a rush. His long wingspan wrapped around her, bundling her up against him, his breath exhaled against her hair at the top of her head. His embrace gave safety and warmth, a nice respite. Hell, she'd started freezing about halfway through her little water charade. "To be honest, Garrett, I didn't even realize what was happening either until after we'd finished. All I noticed was how vanilla it seemed."

He pulled back to look at her. "Vanilla? You smacked me."

"To get us back to what we are." She despised how her words came out on a whisper, exposing her true fear—the worry that tonight might alter who they were somehow, not only to each other, but at their core. In fact, things had already taken a turn for the unknown, and if things continued....

"Honey, we'll always be ourselves. One non-kinky moment won't change that. Did you think I was pissed at you because you hit me?"

"You had a right to be."

He hugged her tight. "As usual, you're dead wrong. Sometimes I wonder where you get some of these crazy ideas. You can hit me all you want because I give as good as I get. My anger came from ignoring my own rules. The ones I expect to follow as much as any other member of the Playroom. We barebacked without discussion, and I'm upset at my lack of control."

Stepping back, Garrett gave her some space, and she giggled when she noticed her soaked dress had left a water tattoo on his shirt and slacks. He glanced down. "Now we're both wet. You're going to pay. But, first, let's talk rules."

Lacey shook her head. "Nope. Did I use my safeword?"

"Rutabaga is hard to mistake for another word, but—"

"Then, that's it. You've decided you won't bareback again without my permission...my consent. Otherwise, you know everything about me. We designed the paperwork together and completed ours before anyone else's. I trust you."

Garrett wrapped her hand in his and lifted it to his lips, pressing a kiss onto the top of her knuckles. "I trust you, too."

Her chest tightened at his response. In their world, such a thing meant more than love, money, or even those so-called friendships where you'd drink a few beers. To give someone trust meant handing over a life, putting it in their possession, and believing they'd cherish it as much as the individual did. Horror stories were common in their circle, from those beaten within an inch of their last breath to a few folks who lost limbs or more. She'd always given her friend the ultimate gift, but never expected him to share the same with her.

He yanked her arm. "Lacey? Honey? Are you okay?"

"Fine." She smiled. "Fine. Tell me what's next, Sir."

Something bothered her, but he'd let it go for now. Deep emotions ran through the room, and, to temper them, he needed to tuck them away fast and furious before the evening became more of a confessional than a scene. She'd ceded control back to him anyway. Her use of "Sir" slayed him each time, making his cock twitch in anticipation.

No point in denying her. "Take off the dress, but leave the heels."

While she undressed, he opened a cabinet drawer and withdrew four flour-sack towels. Since his parents left the house to him three years prior, he'd remodeled everything. Every room tailored to become a playroom of its own. Yet, he didn't have guests, not ones he'd scene with at least. So far, his house had remained untouched from his proclivities, but, with luck, the christening would occur in the next five minutes.

Besides his love for oak cabinets and all appliances made of stainless steel, a center island with a marble counter top stood in the middle of the room. Metal bars had been welded around the top and bottom of this four-foot-long, three-and-a-half-foot-tall prep area. Yes, they'd have fun.

Turning back around, he found her naked. He groaned at her visage. She'd let down her hair, blonde lengths spilling across her shoulders, her pebbled raspberry-colored nipples peeking out between the tresses. Her legs seemed to go on forever, and he planned to touch those first. "Face the island, bend over, spread your legs, and grip the handles on each side."

She did as instructed, a grin on her face. Garrett dangled the towels on his forearm, loving how she hissed as her bare flesh

155

touched the cold marble. He sidestepped the wet, blue mass of material on the floor, and squatted between her legs.

Her arousal scented the air. She smelled salty, an aroma all her own. Before a tasting could occur, punishment needed to be meted out. "You've been bad, Lace."

He looped one towel around each ankle and tied the ends to the metal rods at either side of the block. Once finished, he tapped each leg, encouraging her to move them. If she could, they'd proceed. If not, he'd have to re-tie everything. "Good?"

She pulled against the bindings, secure, but not immobilized. "Perfect, Sir."

Then he did the same thing to her wrists. The sole travesty was he couldn't see her beautiful breasts, but he'd save the pleasure for later. Picking up the dress, he held it over the sink, squeezing the excess water out of the material, the polyester blend perfect for a makeshift flogger.

He loved how Lacey kept turning her head from side to side, attempting to watch his progress, but, thanks to his skills with knots, she possessed limited movement. "Name your favorite color." A question he could guess the answer to. She'd never volunteered the information.

"Chartreuse."

Counting the letters off.... Lucky him. "Ten letters in the name, ten strikes. With ten seconds to rest in between them." The more important determination being where the strikes would hit.

The dress twirled with ease between his hands, and when he let one end snap, it landed on her left cheek.

Crack!

The sound echoed, loud and magical, in the quiet kitchen. She took three deep breaths, followed by slow exhales—using the seconds to process the pain. Yet, he didn't want her calm, and he'd never said what would happen in between strikes. Watching the second hand tick away on the steel clock against the wall, he slid two fingers down the center of her spine as the last three beats of rest concluded. She shivered, and then he struck again, the other cheek this time.

"Are you wet for me?" His hand soothed the area he'd stung then dipped between her legs.

She was wetter than in the truck cab, than even the parking lot.

Obviously, receiving pain suited her as much as giving it. Again, time ticked away, and he sucked her arousal off his fingers. Tangy and he wanted more. After he delivered what he'd promised. Another smack, this time to the back of her thigh.

Instead of another taste, he settled for pinching her clit between his index and middle finger. She let out a short yell, throwing her breathing off. Then the next assault and thus they continued. He'd deliver the blow, following with another offensive on her vagina designed to steal thoughts and concentration.

After the last hit, she begged. "Please."

"Please, what?"

"I need to come."

He laughed. "So do I, but I think you can wait a bit longer." Untying her wrists and ankles, he assisted her in turning around, exposing her breasts to his perusal and granting him easier access to the rest of her body. "In fact, I'm counting on it."

Chapter Five

No words could describe the tingling running through her body, nor the crazy, thrashing impulses she experienced every time the wet fabric hit her. She'd remained calm but didn't stand a chance against Garrett's wandering fingers as he re-secured her ankles in place.

Now that she faced him, she saw his pleasure at her restraint. He loved this, and hell if she didn't find delight in it, too. He leaned in and feasted on her breasts. A true devouring with his tongue and teeth, seeking and coaxing noises from her lips by attacking her sensitive nipples and the surrounding flesh.

He possessed the patience of a saint. She ached to touch him then realized he'd forgotten to secure her arms. She leaned back onto the island with her elbows. His lack of focus implied he'd gotten as lost as she had in the moment.

Before she could grab his head, though, he moved downward, trailing kisses along her belly then bit her side hard, which sent her reeling. The pain, the pleasure—potent and dangerous. He swiped his tongue along her clit. She failed to stop her moan, loud and wanting. A begging plea, in its own way, to have him bring her to orgasm with his mouth.

He didn't wait for her to verbalize her want, just began a fresh attack. Possessing a singular goal to find every nook, touch every piece of flesh in the vicinity, and, if possible, drive rational thought out of her mind. Lacey required release. Without it she'd grow crazy, and who was panting? Shit, that's me.

Her back arched, and she began to crest, but then Garrett pulled away. In a split second, her Dominant nature roared to life. No way in sweet hell would she wait any longer. Hands fisting in his hair, she shoved his mouth back to her, and he followed her lead. As she came, he milked her release from her, sucking every last drop and then lapping at her opening like an animal eager for more. She'd half a mind to demand he screw her right here, charged for a third round.

When she glanced down at him, the grin on her face died. Sparks lit those gray eyes, and he shook his head and clicked his tongue in disapproval. "Naughty girl. You topped from bottom."

She shrugged. "Can you blame me?"

"Yes, I can. I think it's time I familiarized you with my cross."

He released her legs from the towel restraints and eased away into a standing position. "Stay here for a second."

Leaving her hurt like hell, but it would be wrong to have this next conversation with her standing around naked. She'd need some armor, and one of the best kinds could be found in clothes. He traversed the living room in abrupt, fast steps, going into his room and pulling a college T-shirt, Razorback red, from his dresser. No doubt she'd believe him angry with her behavior in the kitchen. Yet, when he owned her release it seemed silly and downright foolish to get pissed about her wanting an orgasm. Therein lay his problem, and he couldn't avoid telling her the truth.

When he entered the kitchen, she stood there, pulling her hair up in a ponytail, a few uneven, shorter strands framing her face. She'd shed the heels, coming down inches, the top of her head just below his chin. "Here's a T-shirt."

"I'm going to need clothes for this next bit?" She sounded surprised but slipped into the garment, and he became jealous of the fabric. He'd love to be the one covering her frame, giving her warmth.

"Yes. You will."

"All right, but it's easier to be naked and strapped to a cross." She walked to him and trailed a hand down his arm. He shoved away the arousal already heating his blood again. Truth be told, there'd never be a time he didn't want this woman. *If she'd just open up to me.*

He chuckled. "I'm afraid you misunderstood. We won't be tying, we'll be talking. My cross is more my burden than anything."

Leading the way, Garrett took her toward his bedroom—his sanctuary. No one had shared this space with him. In fact, outside of friends and family, he almost never brought company to his home. He considered the room he slept in sacred, a safe zone. Fitting he'd tell his past to someone in the one place he found peace—outside of his dungeon. But the Playroom provided a different kind of peace, nothing like here.

Lacey followed, fingers from one hand wrapped up in his. The warmth, the touch buoyed him. Made him believe in the rightness of what he'd been pursuing with her all night. When they reached the doorway, he stopped, giving her a chance to look around. From the four poster, cedar, king-size bed to the floor-to-ceiling windows overlooking his back patio and the land beyond. Her mouth dropped open.

"Better close your mouth, or I'll put something in it," he said, with a wink.

"Ha. I'll believe that when I see it." She crossed the threshold and paused again. "Hell, Garrett. You never told me about this. Like you never told me about Logan."

"Like... I didn't tell you a lot of things." In ways, their friendship could be viewed as superficial. Yet, it ran deeper in other aspects. Favorite things, kink preferences, food selections, and even philosophies were similar. He'd been the shoulder to cry on, the one who'd jump-start her car or rescue her from unwanted situations.

A frown marred her face then changed to one of the thinking variety. "What else haven't you bothered to share?"

Here we go. "Did I ever tell you how I came into BDSM?"

"No."

No surprise. He'd kept this story to himself for the longest time. "Then it's good you're here because I'm ready to tell someone. Sit down, please."

She took cautious steps, as if trying to decide if she wanted to go through this. Regardless, she made it to the bed and bounced on the edge with her bottom. "Springy. I like it."

"I do, too." Garrett ran a hand through his hair and sighed.

"Just say it. It's like I tell my patients. If you're experiencing pain, the best way to fix it is to confess the pain to begin with." Leave it to Lacey to make it simple.

"All right. My first experience with BDSM was as a submissive."

She didn't appear shocked, so he continued.

"It happened in high school with a college girl. We went to a party at some house. Free booze and older women. Some hot chick approached me and asked what I would do to see her tits. I told her

I'd let her do whatever she wanted. That was the beginning of the end for me."

She shrugged. "So, you got introduced to the lifestyle by some college chick. Doesn't sound so horrible."

"Here's the thing. It's not horrible, but I'm not a true Dominant. I'm a switch. Even then, I'm not solely bound to the lifestyle. I can enjoy sex without following strict kink or even involving kink at all. A little bonus option never hurt anything, but...." He hoped letting his sentence hang in the air that she'd get his meaning.

"Are you confessing because somehow this is supposed to make me regret things? You've been fighting for something sexual, intimate between us all night. I've been giving in and giving it up. Now, you've changed your mind?"

Damn. What a horrible job of explaining what he'd done. A downright shitty job. "That's not the reason for my confession. I don't want you to regret anything. I want you to realize I can tell you're not submitting. You're riding the line of dominance, a thin line, but there's no crossing it."

"I let you spank me." She stood, back arched and hard nipples outlined by the fabric of the shirt. "I let you tie me down and finger bang me in a public parking lot."

"And you got off in return. Give and take. You gave for the reward I bestowed. Not for the sake of it." He shivered when her eyes narrowed at his words. She noticed. How fucking horrible to have his traitor body succumbing to her. She'd take advantage of him and no doubt he'd let her. Fuck.

Instinct told her Garrett wanted to submit, and she only needed to command him to do so. Except...he'd asked her for submission. For this one thing and one chance. So far, she'd done a half-assed job. She gave a little then took an equal amount back. In fact, the parking lot episode proved more a steam release than anything.

The evening, so far, had shown her best friend played the role of lover well. He accommodated, protected, and worried about her safety, her pleasure. Maybe this once she could, in all honesty, let go. Trust in him to the fullest extent, as he'd just trusted her with his most guarded secret.

"Fine. Do with me what you want, but when it's my turn" — she licked her lips — "you're going to be begging."

"Are you for real this time?"

"No taking advantage. No reacting out of turn or topping from bottom. I'll be the perfect submissive." Jumping off the bed, she assumed the position on the floor, supplicating herself in front of him.

"Then look at the floor and stay silent until I tell you otherwise."

She stared at the rug beneath her. Multi-colored woven fabric, handmade, and soft instead of scratchy. No doubt the hardwood floors underneath would soon begin to hurt her knees, even with the rug as a buffer. Garrett's footsteps trailed out of the room. She heard a light switch, running water, and — crap!

If he'd decided to take a shower, she was stuck here, waiting. How she'd love to get up, march in there, and turn the water cold. Chilling him to the bone then ply his forgiveness with hot towels and the promise of her mouth on his cock — but only if he begged.

However, she'd chosen to submit. A path leaving her doomed to wait until he decided she deserved his attention.

Chapter Six

Garrett chose a true test for Lacey. Patience. She'd never exhibited much during their training, unless she was the one in charge. Then she had the patience of a hen waiting for her eggs to hatch. So, he'd decided to clean up, washing the earlier events of the evening away with a little body wash and a loofah. The hot water relaxed his muscles. When he emerged from the tiled shower, his skin tingled with the urge to fall at her feet and ask her to trade places. No one else but she triggered his desire to submit, always had. He'd trained her and been jealous of the men and women she got under her boots.

He needed to shove his fears and submissive tendencies aside to withstand what the next few hours would hold. No more switching behavior. He needed to embrace the dominant side of himself because he'd been less focused on the scene and more on being with her any way she'd have him.

He'd also reached another conclusion while soaping himself down in the shower. He'd fallen in love with his best friend. She challenged, conquered, and commanded his entire being. He needed to keep any declarations of love to himself until the morning. This time, he would not stop until she broke. Until she pleaded.

He walked out of the bathroom, naked and ready to begin. Surprise rolled through him—Lacey still held position on the floor, head bowed. "Are you awake?"

Without raising her head, she replied, "Yes, Sir."

"Good." He grabbed a blindfold from the top of his dresser and placed it over her eyes. "Rise."

She pushed herself up and stood, a neutral expression on her face. He wrapped his hand around her upper arm and guided her to the bed.

"Hop up there, lie on your back, and put your arms over your head."

So far, she performed admirably, and when he shackled her

163

wrists in bondage cuffs, securing them to his headboard, she stayed calm. In fact, she practiced the breathing techniques they'd both taught dozens of subs over the years. Meditation practices designed to relax the body in the first moments of a scene, to prepare for the more challenging parts. Then Garrett added the element of the spreader bar, locking it to her ankles and exposing her to him.

The T-shirt of his alma mater still covered her. To amp things up, he sliced it open with a small knife. The sound of the fabric splitting rent the air, and she took a sharp intake of breath. The red material fell open on either side, exposing those gorgeous breasts of hers, nipples already hard and at attention. He trailed the dull side of the knife around each nipple, loving how she shivered as cold metal met warm flesh. Then he tucked the instrument away, replacing metal with his tongue. Each point received five seconds of individual attention via his mouth . She moaned and cried out when he pulled away.

When he skimmed his fingernails in across her skin, near her stomach, arms, and upper thighs, she squirmed and thrashed against the sensations. The phantom feelings such touches left on the little hairs of the skin acted as effective as the strikes from a whip or paddle. Determined to drive her insane, he chose to employ softer, gentler methods.

Those involved massage oil and his palms kneading into her flesh, working away the tension coiled in each muscle. Garrett started at her feet and moved upward. The slow, meticulous process brought a new level of sensuality into the scene. He'd never spent this much time on a body before. Sure, massages played a role with clients, but, at most, he stuck to one body part or area due to time. In Lacey's case, he had all night.

Once done with her upper thighs, he slid his fingertips over her labia. Not penetrating and relishing her frustrated sigh. He moved to the chest, even her breasts, the collarbone, the shoulders, and her neck. Then he pressed kisses to her eyes, nose, and cheeks.

"Please," she whispered, arching her back and thrusting her breasts in the air. He savored the way they brushed against his body. The initial begging was always the quietest and most insincere.

So, he grabbed a pillow, placing it under her back, right where her spine curved, elevating her body off the bed. The cuffs and spreader bar still held her at his mercy. He put his mouth to use on her body, nibbling the sensitive areas of skin. At her neck, her stomach, and near her hips. She'd sigh then take a sharp inhale at different intervals, as well as worry her bottom lip with those perfect white teeth of hers. When he reached her thighs, she moaned, "I need you to fuck me."

"I need you to fuck me...?"

"Sir?" The word came out more a question, a damned exasperated one.

"Sir...?"

She frowned then clenched her legs shut around the hand he had rested between them. "I need release, please. I'm begging you. No more torture, Sir. Set me free."

Desperation. He'd accept such a thing. He freed her ankles from the spreader bar then grabbed a condom from the drawer. Sheathing his cock, he seated himself between her legs, positioned to enter the one place she wanted him. Before he did, though, he wanted to make eye contact. He pulled the blindfold down, turning it into a gag. Aquamarine, lust-filled eyes met his own. "Are you comfortable? Nod once for yes or shake your head for no."

She nodded.

"We'll make love, not fuck." Then he slid home. Her tight, wet passage gripped him, and he groaned when he pulled out. He controlled the situation with slow, measured, penetrating strokes. A steady and agonizing way to reach an orgasm, but it would occur all the same. He took those moments to memorize the body of the woman he loved. "I want to worship you. Not treat you as a means to an end. You're gorgeous, precious."

She shook her head.

"Don't deny what I tell you. Whatever I say is the truth. It exists here and now, with us." He pulled out at a snail's pace, enjoying the natural edges and bumps to their anatomy and each one drove him a little closer. Plunging back in, Garrett quickened the pace a little, leaning down to move the blindfold with his teeth. With the scrap of material out of the way, their lips met. What started as slow, tender kisses dissolved into eager tongues and nipping teeth.

He needed this, the closeness and the passion behind the kisses. Whether she'd admit it or not, her feelings ran deeper than friendship. Evidenced by the way she rushed back to kiss him again and again. As if one or a thousand would ever be enough.

They broke apart as the pressure built. If anything, his cock held more rigidity than before, and when she tensed against his body, feet locking behind his back, the dam burst. He cried out her name, as she did his, and they both came together. A rush of emotions swamped him—from satisfaction to a primal need to shout out his love. He fought the urge at the same time his body jerked with the last vestiges of his orgasm.

Looking at her face, he brushed a few tendrils of blonde hair away, and she smiled. He admired how their activity had put a healthy flush to her cheeks and a thin sheen of sweat on her brow. "Lace, I…. Give me two seconds." That's all he'd need to hop off the bed and discard the condom. A close one, Rogers.

"Wait. Can you let me out of the cuffs first? My arms are a bit strained." She shook said arms, and the chains attached to his headboard clinked against each other.

He leaned in and pressed a tender kiss to her forehead. "Sure thing."

Once he'd removed the cuffs, he straightened. "Now, don't you move. I'm going to the bathroom for a minute then I will be back to take care of you. Rest, relax."

Hell, if the condom hadn't been in his hand, he would've clapped with joy. She'd embraced submission without fault, and showed him an equal amount of passion with a zeal matching his own for her. The rest of the evening could be spent with him enjoying her aftercare. A few hot towels to soothe her lower arms, wrists, and ankles. Then some fruit and water as a treat, served bedside. Holding and snuggling might come into play. He'd turned into a damn sap.

But, as he looked at himself in the bathroom mirror, the smile on his face refused to diminish. Running a few washcloths under hot water in the sink, he kept grinning and thinking. When he had four towels ready, he shut off the water and walked back into the bedroom. The only problem was his submissive and best friend no longer lay on the bed.

"Lacey," he called out. Setting the towels on the bathroom counter, he headed to the living room. When he found it empty, he proceeded to the kitchen. No Lacey there, either.

When he looked out the window, he found his truck missing.

She had to get out of there, and the way out involved taking Garrett's truck. She grabbed her purse from where she'd tossed it next to her on the seat and fished her cell phone out one-handed. Bless the heavens for speed dial. A press of one button and her sister's voice called out to her after two rings.

"What's up, big sis?"

"Are you home?" Good chance she sounded paranoid or freaked out. Her hand, holding the wheel, trembled a little.

"No, in fact, I'm not even in the continental United States. Remember, Kanoa and I are on the islands, visiting his family. I'm doing the meet-the-parents thing and, thank goodness, I've survived. In fact, I don't think I want to come home. This place is gorgeous—"

"Great. I'm glad you're having an awesome time. I won't hold you up." The word gorgeous…. Fuck, any word with ties to pretty, breathtaking, or beautiful.

"Are you okay?" Laney's voiced dropped lower. "If you need me home, say the word and I'm on a flight."

She cringed at her selfishness and the deep desire to say yes. Her sister had never rescued her a day in her life—not until a few months ago when she went on a 1Night Stand date on her behalf. The date had changed Laney's life, for the better. She refused to ruin her little sister's vacation with her boyfriend because she couldn't cope with a scene.

"I'm fine. I'll call Garrett or someone to help me out. You enjoy the beaches, the ocean, and the sunshine." She applied the brakes, coming to halt at the end of the dirt road. A right or left turn onto asphalt remained in front of her.

"If you're sure. Don't hesitate to call me back if you change your mind." Having a twin made it difficult to have secrets or to keep them.

"I will. Bye." She didn't wait for a response, just pressed the red button, ended the call, and sat there for a moment, staring into the dark. A runner. God, she'd become a wimp. A laugh gurgled out of her mouth, followed by a sob. She brought her hand up to stifle the sound. What should have been a simple stress reliever, a test of their attraction to one another, had turned into another beast all together.

Add in how he'd made love to her…. Yep, he'd picked turns of phrase she'd never associated with sex. Love meant feelings of a personal nature. He'd whispered sweet nothings, called her things no man ever dared.

Her phone buzzed then belted out Sam Smith's "Like I Can," interrupting her silent musings. Garrett's name lit up the screen, along with an image of him grinning, those stormy grays shining at her. No way in hell would she pick up. He'd get his truck back tomorrow after she had time to get her shit together.

Pressing the silent button on the phone, she held down the power key and shut the damn thing off. Peace and quiet would be the order for the rest of the night.

She turned the truck left, pointed east, and headed toward home.

Chapter Seven

For the first ten minutes, he tried not to freak out, even ignored the fact she'd stolen his truck just to escape the house. When she didn't answer the phone, he got a little worried. Subsequent calls went straight to voice mail. His worry meter went off the charts.

It took him fifteen more minutes to get a cab company on the phone to come pick him up. They'd said it would be a bit due to some last minute flights and an increase requests for the late night. He'd never known the area to be so busy at one in the morning. He'd half a mind to call Laney as he sat on his couch, waiting. Flipping his phone over and over in his hand, he contemplated bringing little sister into the mess. The situation called for it—he'd created a fucking disaster zone.

The cab pulled up and honked before he could give in to temptation. He grabbed his leather jacket, a shield against the chilly night air, and jumped into the backseat of his ride. The shitty part was it'd been over an hour since Lacey took off— plus, another thirty minutes spent getting lost on the ride into town, helping the new-to-the-job driver find her house, and paying the man who drove for the sole non-credit-card-accepting company in the area with every last dollar bill he had on him.

When, at last, he stood on the front stoop, the porch light casting a dull yellow halo around him, he hesitated, hand raised midair, doubt swamping his gut. She'd run for a reason. Maybe he should let her have time to herself. Let her think things through. But then he glanced at his truck in her driveway. A reminder she'd run from him, refused to talk to him, or even explain what the hell happened. He'd been worried about her safety, her life. Relief at seeing his black truck parked at her house helped let the rock in his gut disappear, but an angry belly fire replaced it.

He both rang the doorbell and pounded on the door multiple times. After the third round, the front door popped open, and she poked her head out. "What do you want, Garrett?"

"My keys for starters, and then maybe letting me in so you can explain why you stole my truck and went running, unless you want the neighbors getting the whole story, too."

She glanced around, taking in the lack of attentive neighbors and his empty threat. For a second, it seemed like she'd refuse, but then she stepped back, opening the door with her. "Come on in."

"Thank you."

He heard the dead bolt click, and turned on her before they could reach the living room. "What in the sweet hell, Lace? You almost killed me."

"Can I get you a drink?" She crossed her arms over the front of the Bugs Bunny T-shirt that hung past her knees.

Unbelievable. "I need something that's not water." He took off his leather jacket and hung it on a coat hook in the hall before stalking into the living room and plopping on her couch. He shoved his hands into his hair—surprised he still had some after tugging on it multiple times on the way over.

She came back in the room, carrying two glasses of amber liquid, ice cubes tinkling against crystal with each step she took. He hoped.... "Bourbon?"

"Yes, a little Beam." She held one glass out to him.

He grabbed it and shot back a healthy mouthful, exhaling as it slid down his throat like his daddy taught him. "Thank you. Ready to talk?" They would discuss this even if he had to hound her until the sun came up.

"I think so." She sat next to him, pushing her untouched glass onto the table. "I freaked out."

"A little hard not to notice."

Sighing, she tugged the oversized T-shirt over her legs and then hugged them. "You said things I wasn't ready for. Did things—"

Chuckling, he touched her, embracing the spark, the tingle a result of the action. She froze, but he kept on, sliding a finger up and down her arm. "Precious, you've never danced around a subject with me yet. Don't start now, please?"

She pulled away from him. "Fine. You called what we did making love. An important part of the conversation you failed to mention. I never agreed to it. Never wanted it."

If those words weren't a mood killer—and hurtful. "Yet, you never used your safeword."

"I'm using it now. Rutabaga."

Two hours ago, he would've called everything to a halt. But now? "This isn't a scene. We're in a conversation, and we'll talk things through."

Lacey looked up with tears in her eyes. "I'm scared."

"Have you taken a shower?" Always his first suggestion in times of stress. Running water, especially warm, tended to relax tension.

She nodded, and tear drops fell, splashing against her T-shirt, running down her face.

He set his glass next to hers. "Precious, can I touch you?"

She launched herself at him. He wrapped his arms around her, pulling her tight against his body and burying his face in her hair. Damp hair smelling like flowers, a scent he'd never forget. "You should have stayed and let me take care of you."

"People don't take care of me," she mumbled against his shirt. "It's my job."

"Yes, but we shared a scene, and you broke the rules. Why?" Rules she'd known and always obeyed. In fact, her aftercare was as famous as her sensory deprivation sessions.

"I told you, I got scared. What you're after is more than I'm capable of giving."

He squeezed her against him. "From what I can tell, you gave without issue, and I think you desired what happened as much as I did. If you can tell me you hated every moment of our scene, or that you faked your orgasms, then I'll leave. No harm, no foul."

"It has nothing to do with not liking it or the orgasms. The intimacy is the part I can't handle."

What? "You've been intimate with many people, and I don't think it's a horrible thing at all. In fact, you're a pro."

Lacey scooted away from him then, with a self-deprecating smile. "Here's the thing. I'm a fake."

She didn't relish the confusion marring Garrett's face, nor did she like the idea of airing all her dirty laundry. Yet, he'd shared his secrets with her.... She owed him the same.

"My scenes don't involve intimacy. It's like a job for me. The only difference is that sometimes, when I choose, I'll get orgasms

171

out of the deal. I'm not good at relinquishing control. Men don't date me for very long because I tend to take things over. The last real boyfriend I had was in college about two weeks before I met you. He ditched me when he caught me sorting his laundry. I've gotten better over the years, but even Laney…. We share a house and she gives me wide berth. The only room off-limits to my fanatic ways is her bedroom. Then there's the fact I liked to call the shots on where we ate, having oral sex, and a dozen other things my past boyfriends complained about."

Garrett shook his head, no doubt at her insanity. "What does this have to do with intimacy?"

"I pretended. I'm a good actress. Sure I get off on being in control, it satisfies my more attention-to-detail obsessive urges, but at the end of the day I don't give any of myself to the subs in my care. My dates never made it past question number five of my requirements. Most of them, while gentlemen, had too many caveman tendencies for me to be able to trust them." She sounded nuts, at least her sister had told her half a dozen times she did.

"Yes, but you gave it to me." He whispered the words before reaching for his glass on the coffee table and downing the rest of the bourbon. "As for the other stuff, I don't give a shit."

Her jaw dropped open, and a thread of anger found a home in her veins. She wiped the tracks of tears from both cheeks and growled, "Way to be sensitive."

He cradled her face with an open palm. "I don't care about those things because I've always loved those things about you. You know what you want all the time. No doubts, no second-guessing. When I ask you questions you give answers. Organizing, scheduling, and keeping things super clean are a few things I'm a stickler at, too. As for intimacy, can't you feel it?"

Fingers traced over her features, resting against her lips, and the heat from those two tips on her flesh spread throughout her body without additional provocation. She'd felt things during the course of the evening she'd not often experienced with others. From his emotions, to the strong ones she inspired in him. "I do. You're not mad?" Her lips pressed against those fingers, and he shivered before pulling them away.

"About what?"

"Me leaving."

He shook his head. "I'm more upset you left and didn't tell me where you went. I think the worst was when you wouldn't pick up the phone."

Scared for her well-being. In ways, she'd acted more selfish in that moment than she'd ever been. "I'm sorry for freaking you out. Thank you for coming after me."

"I would've come after you no matter what."

Moments ticked by as they stared at one another. The silence increased the awkwardness. Garrett had proved there was no going back to the way things were. In ways, she found herself thankful to be entering something new. In others, she cursed the whole damn evening. How to fix this? How to ask the question someone needed to ask?

She took a swallow of bourbon to summon the courage. "What next?"

"Whatever you desire. I'm yours. I've been yours for years, just didn't know it."

"You're the one talking crazy now."

"Am I?" He grinned. "You can ask anything. Demand it and I'll do it." Intent lay with his words and she meant to challenge them.

"Fine. Strip."

"As you wish." He stood from the couch and peeled off his T-shirt first.

Before he dropped it to the floor, she issued another edict. "Fold every article and place it on the table. I don't want a mess."

He nodded in acknowledgement and neatly folded each piece of clothing as he removed it, forming a small stack. She watched him the whole time, taking in the muscles, the varying tones of skin based on the parts left exposed to the sun and the ones covered by clothing all the time, as well as his general physique. All the elements in tandem left her hot and bothered by the time he finished, and he let her look her fill. In fact, no comment, not even heavy breathing, came from his direction. She got up and cupped his erection in her hands, as if weighing him, and he grew hard at her touch. The inspection continued, checking every inch of skin for a blemish, a varicose vein, and, at last, his teeth. Those pearly whites appeared perfect, thanks to her hounding and his regular dentist trips. In fact, his entire body appeared tuned and in great shape.

"I'd say you're sufficient." No sense in giving too high praise.

"Thank you, Ma'am." He smiled wide, his Southern twang a little more prominent.

She tapped his shoulder. "Don't thank me yet. Follow me to the bedroom."

They traversed the small hallway, passing by her sister's mess of a room and the small office they shared, until they got to the last door. Her desire to see Garrett's reaction to her personal space surprised her. No man had ever entered, so she walked backward into the room, flipping the light switch to turn on three lamps in three of the four corners. She'd settled on a purple motif, from the draped, sheer violet fabric hanging across the four-poster bed to the multi-shaded purple comforter, matching rugs on the wooden floor, and painted white furniture.

"Very elegant," he said, walking inside until he stood in front of her bed — a feminine room invaded by overwhelming masculinity and testosterone.

"It's not girly." She'd never apologized for her sense of style, but thanks to the intimacy doors being flung open, her emotions rode close to the surface.

"No, it's you. I like it." He glanced around then back at her. "Where do you want me?"

"On the bed."

"Any particular way?" Damn him for being so accommodating and willing to ask her preference in the littlest of things.

Grinning, she remembered one particular punishment she wanted to enact before going to bed. "Wait one minute."

Turning, she dug into the top drawer of her dresser, searching for her play box. Sure, she never entertained at home, but she'd invested in a box of personal instruments in case the day ever came. "Aha!" She turned around, holding up the clear cock ring.

His smile turned wary.

"Don't tell me you've never worn one of these."

"It's been a while." Yet, no complaint, no objection or safing out. He let her slide the ring down his shaft to the base. Due to the focus needed in keeping him safe, she lost out on the pleasure of watching his facial expressions, except she'd been the lucky recipient of one low growl as his cock pulsed, thanks in part to her fingertips.

"Perfect. Pull the comforter back and climb on in."

She walked off to her master bathroom, brushed her hair, her teeth then returned to the sight of him touching himself. Slow, languid strokes and he groaned when he saw her. Climbing into bed, she almost gave in, almost let herself lose control, but she didn't want sex. No, such a thing could wait.

"Stop teasing yourself. There will be no orgasming for you anytime soon."

He let go of his cock and rested his head on the pillows. "You're going to kill me."

"No, I'm going to ask you questions, and then we are going to sleep." She stripped off her shirt and folded it before placing it on her nightstand shelf. His body already warmed the sheets, but she still shivered.

"No good, Lacey. I can't let you go cold. May I get close to you?"

She nodded. "Before today, how often did you share a bed with someone?"

"Never, at least not at my house. I've shared a bed with a few women, but always in the dungeon or in their homes. Until tonight, no woman had been in my room."

Ironic. "Funny, I can say the same about this room. This is my space as well. I don't share it with anyone else. No man has been in here."

"Now, you're willing to share it with me?" He chuckled, pulling the purple silk sheet and comforter over them. Then his arms reached for her, and she went, seeking the comfort, the safety he could offer.

Sighing, she relaxed into him. "I can't explain it, but you brought up valid points about intimacy and how you accept me. I thought this was the next logical step, seeing if we slept well together. Plus, not to push up your ego, but I'm exhausted."

"Then sleep, precious. Let's see how this works."

Chapter Eight

G arrett woke with a start, almost jumping out of his skin at the touch of a warm, graceful hand encircling his cock.

"It's okay, manly man. You're here with me."

A glance told him Lacey's intent gaze watched him. "How long have you been up?"

"About fifteen minutes." A solid stroke on his cock accompanied each word. What a way to wake up. "During that time, I realized two things. One, you don't hog the covers, and two, you smile in your sleep."

"I do?" The last thing he remembered dreaming about eluded him, replaced with the sensations racking his body, thanks to her attentions. "I can't really recall."

"Well, I can think of another way to put a smile on your face." She stripped back the sheet, exposing them both. "Oral."

Damn. He loved her enthusiasm. If she changed her mind after today, he'd break, knowing he'd lose out on waking up to future mornings of this. She climbed on top of him, aligning her glistening vagina, ready for him. He tongued once, testing the waters, and her answering plea told him he'd found the right spot. Judging from the attention, albeit torture and teasing, she applied to his cock, there would be pleasure for both of them. Her strokes and tongue massaged him in a slow, maddening dance. The exception being, he couldn't come until she removed the ring.

The best course would be to get her to orgasm as quickly as possible. So, he penetrated her channel, mimicking what he wanted to do to her with other anatomy parts. Then he traced her labia, before moving to her clit. She'd never said fingers were off-limits, so he inserted two digits as his tongue assaulted her in a series of flicks and lapping. He could tell she was close by the way her core constricted around him, clenching his fingers. She came with a scream, and the vibration had him arching his back, but she refused to remove him from her mouth.

Her legs trembled, and she sat up, releasing her hold on him. "Hot Jesus, if I didn't want you inside me so bad, I'd make you do that again."

The cock ring came off, but then he remembered he'd come without protection—condoms being the last thing on his mind last night when he only worried about her safety. "We can if you want. I didn't bring any protection with me."

"Lucky for you, I've got some. An unopened box, in fact." She crawled off the bed, rummaging in her dresser drawer again. When she emerged, she held a foil packet. "In case my one-night stand came back to my place…. Not a plan, but I hoped things would go a bit further."

After ripping it open, she rolled the condom on, and he groaned. "Wait."

"What?"

He'd kill the mood, but there was no help for it. "I can't do this until I tell you I love you, and last night, this morning, everything is so wonderful. If you tell me after this we can't continue, or we won't explore things…."

She leaned in and kissed him, a sweet butterfly kiss that turned into hardcore frenching within seconds. When they broke apart, panting, she smacked his face. "I love you, too. And don't even think about it. I'm not letting you go."

Relief swamped him, adding a heightened sense to his arousal as she climbed onto the bed and straddled him. She impaled herself on his cock, letting their bodies get accustomed to one another again. As delicious as the first time they'd done it in his truck. He fully expected each time to be like this, hoped for it, and silently promised himself to work to keep her happy.

"I'm on top," she said with a grin.

"Whatever you desire."

About Landra Graf

Landra Graf consumes at least one book a day, and has always been a sucker for stories where true love conquers all. She believes in the power of the written word, and the joy such words can bring. In between spending time with her family and having book adventures, she writes romance with the goal of giving everyone, fictional or not, their own happily ever after.

describe the kind of sex she longed for. "Don't be gentle, pound into me."

A twist of his hips and she rolled underneath him. He used his elbows to balance himself and then acted on her commands. Her breath whooshed out of her body each time he entered, as if forcibly pulled from her. A tight, spiraling feeling, deep in her core, rose fast and ever elusive. "I'm almost there."

Kanoa's lips touched hers then his tongue. The connection, somehow, brought everything to a head, her orgasm cresting as he pulled out slowly. She clenched around him, trying to stop his exit, but he broke their kiss. "If I stay, I'll break your rule."

"Then break it." She needed to feel his release, to watch him come undone while inside her.

The response to her request involved entering her again. Nothing neat or composed, but a wild, mad pace in which he lifted her off the bed by a couple of inches, arching her body back. The head of his cock touched some special part inside her and his breathing sounded strained. She leaned up and licked his nipple. He shuddered in response then lost it. Control gone, his body jerked against hers, and she came again. Involuntarily, unable to stop the primitive reaction.

When he let her go, gently placing her back on the bed, all action ceased. They stared at each other, lost for moment. The evidence of what they'd done hit her. Experiencing release...together...something she'd rarely achieved with other partners. He'd exposed her to a huge number of firsts tonight and had stripped away the mechanisms she'd used to protect herself for so long.

"Let me get you some water." Kanoa's words broke their connection, jarring her back to reality. She had the urge to cover herself. *The exhibitionist turning shy. Lacey would laugh her ass off.*

"Sounds good." Laney pulled the top sheet loose on the bed and climbed underneath it. When he came back with not only a bottle of water but a plate of strawberry-topped cheesecake, too, her heart melted a little more. Whether she lived to regret it or not, he'd be stuck with her for a while.

"We never did get dessert, and I found this in the fridge. Courtesy of my friends, I'm sure. Didn't know if you wanted the champagne." He set the plate on the nightstand and opened her bottle of water.

She shook her head. "No, just the water."

After she took her drink, he extended a fork with a bite of cheesecake. "My mother would never forgive me if I didn't let the lady take the first bite."

She opened her mouth in reception. The silky, smooth texture of the cake and the sweet strawberry topping had her eyes rolling to the back of her head. "It's delicious. Tell me, do your mother's teachings rule most of your interactions?"

"Not always." He ate a bite of dessert. "In this situation, she'd demand I make an honest woman out of you."

She smiled. "Old-fashioned to the core, huh?"

"A bit, but she always means well." He fed her another bite, and, as she chewed, crazy thoughts and images swirled in her brain. Of a wedding on a Hawaiian beach, their friends around them, and the sun setting. Thoughts about a house, and Kanoa wrestling two children, both having his tan skin and her blonde hair.

"Would it be so crazy?"

"What?" He raised an eyebrow.

Time to take the plunge. She'd most likely end up with a fresh dose of reality plus humility on her head, but.... "Marrying me. Loving me. Staying forever with me."

The fork fell from his hand and clattered against the plate.

Fuck. She'd misjudged, maybe misread everything. A kiss did not a marriage make, and she'd probably scared him off. Forget her sister taking ridiculous risks; she'd plunged off the deep end. "Never mind, forget I asked."

"We just met." He glanced at the bedside clock. "About seven hours ago. It's a little quick to jump to those decisions. Not saying I haven't had some crazy thoughts myself in the last little bit."

She waved her hand in the air in agreement. Marriage could be considered jumping the gun in a big way, time to slow it down. "How about a relationship? Is it too farfetched?"

More silence and she wanted to swallow back her words, her blunt honesty and eagerness to blurt out what she wanted. At the same time, it had needed to be said. "You're killing me with the quiet. Talk to me. Tell me what you think."

He pursed his lips and shook his head then laughed. "I think you're a dream come true, and I'm willing to take the chance if you are."

"Mission accepted."

What You Desire

Dedication

To all the boys I loved before, thanks for letting me go so I could find the one man I'm willing to give up control to.

What You Desire

Lacey Malcolm is searching for the one...
She wants a submissive who will love her and all the bad habits she has, including her OCD tendencies.

Second time is the charm...
Her first shot at a 1Night Stand date went wrong when she got ill and sent her sister in her place. With another chance, she's sure this time things will work out.

He's fallen hard...
Garrett Rogers has been Lacey's best friend since college. Only in the last few months has he realized she's the one he wants. Not wanting to risk losing his opportunity, he seeks Madame Eve's help. The date is set, but when he shows up, things may not go as planned since he's asking her to trade in her dominance for one night of submission.